COP'S KID

COP'S KID

by Scott Corbett

Illustrated by
Jo Polseno

An Atlantic Monthly Press Book
Little, Brown and Company
Boston   Toronto

LIBRARY OF CONGRESS CATALOG CARD NO. 68–12347

FIRST EDITION

ATLANTIC–LITTLE, BROWN BOOKS
ARE PUBLISHED BY
LITTLE, BROWN AND COMPANY
IN ASSOCIATION WITH
THE ATLANTIC MONTHLY PRESS

Published simultaneously in Canada
by Little, Brown & Company (Canada) Limited

PRINTED IN THE UNITED STATES OF AMERICA

COP'S KID

1

CHIP WAS SITTING at the kitchen table, growling over his homework. Supper was long past. In no time at all now it would be bedtime. He broke the point of his pencil and said something about it before he could catch himself. He hoped his mother had not heard, but of course she had. A beagle or even a bat could not outhear a mother when it came to hearing something she shouldn't. Hands on hips, she turned on him from the sink.

"Chip Brady! What kind of language is that?"

"Aw, Mom, that's not even bad! You ought to hear some of the guys when they get going."

"I've heard them, and I wouldn't give houseroom to the lot of them. Or if I did, they'd soon straighten out, after your father had given them the back of his hand a few times. Now, what's going on? Are you still working on that same problem?"

"Yes, and I'm going to keep on till I get it!" he snapped, reminding her of his father. He hadn't been a year old before his Uncle Frank had hung that "chip off the old block" nickname on him, but his uncle had been right.

"I wish I could help," she said, "but I don't understand this new math they give you today. Maybe when your father gets home —"

"Pop says he doesn't understand it either."

Mrs. Brady sighed.

"Things were easier when I was in school. Parents could still help you with your homework!"

At his end of the table, Benny tossed down his pencil and sat back looking relieved.

"Well, there's that old book report all done," he announced. "What a job!"

Chip gave him a lordly glance.

"You don't know what homework is, in the fifth grade. Wait till you get to the seventh!"

But Benny was not taking in these words of wisdom. He had jumped up and gone to the window, which was half covered with frost patterns.

"Boy, look at the way it's snowing! Mom, you know what I'd like to do? I'd like to go out and walk in the snow while it's still fresh! Can we go out for just a little while?"

"Benny, it's almost your bedtime, and besides, I don't like you to be out on the streets after dark."

"Aw, Mom, we'll be careful!"

Chip joined his brother at the window for a look. Big snowflakes were falling fast, blanketing the city. Everything was white and beautiful. The small, well-kept houses along their block looked like Christmas card scenes. There was not a mark in the snow. Nobody was out, not a car was in sight.

"Take your books off the table, Benny, so I can set a place for your father. He ought to be home any minute." He was on late duty, and they had eaten supper without him. Mrs. Brady opened the refrigerator, and Benny was in luck. "Oh, darn!"

"Watch your language, Mom!"

"Chip, you stop being so fresh."

"What's wrong?"

"I forgot to get cream for your father's coffee."

"We'll go to the store!"

"Well . . . Are they still open? It's nearly nine."

The Bradys lived in a second-floor flat. From the kitchen window they could see clear over into Stedman Square, if they stood on the right-hand side and looked out sideways toward the left.

"I can see lights on," said Chip, eager now to go outside, too.

"Well, all right, I'll let you run to the store for me —"

"And can we stay out for a little while?"

"Yes, a little while. But I want you back here in ten minutes."

"Ten minutes? Aw —"

"And be careful!"

"Don't worry, there isn't even one car out."

"One could always come along, and it only takes

one, so you watch out. Bundle up, now, and wear your boots."

Two minutes later they were outside and rolling down the little terrace in front of their house. When they had picked themselves up, and tested the snow for its snowball qualities, they tramped down the middle of the street, enjoying the chance to have it to themselves, enjoying the quiet, muffled, half-seen world around them. Here and there streetlamps threw a pale golden circle of light on the snow, their glow dimmed by the swirling flakes. Ahead of them, in the center of Stedman Square, the park's five or six small trees were rapidly becoming a good deal better looking than usual. Under them the benches where old men sat and gossiped in the summertime were mounded with snow.

A snowplow had already been through the square, because it was the end of the line for a couple of bus routes. From there the buses swung around the little park and went back again up Milford Avenue. As the boys neared the square a bus came lumbering into it. In the snowstorm even the bus seemed to make less noise than usual.

"Hey, that's Mr. Fader," said Chip. Because they lived at the end of the line, they knew lots of the bus drivers. Mr. Fader was one they liked. "Let's go ask him how he's making out in the snow."

The bus moved past the intersection and out of sight. It had only one passenger, a tall man in a tan jacket with

its fur-lined collar turned up around his face. He had got to his feet and was busy lighting a cigarette, bracing himself in the aisle while he lit it. Chip and Benny turned the corner and trailed after the bus.

When they padded through the snow alongside it, they could see that the passenger was still on the bus, talking to Mr. Fader. Then everything became like a dream, like a nightmare. First Chip caught a glimpse of Mr. Fader's face, turned up at the passenger. It was white. Next he saw the gun in the man's hand. For a second Chip's heart seemed to stop, turning him into a statue that could not do anything but stare. Then he found his voice and yelled.

"Help! Police! Help!"

His father. If only his father —

The man with the gun must have gotten the surprise of his life. He spun around, staring wildly, and the whole thing seemed more nightmarish than ever, because his face was a ridiculous, half-witted, grinning thing with a couple of chipmunk teeth in the middle of it and the cigarette dangling out of his mouth under them. With a sort of panicky snarl he jumped off the bus straight at them. Both boys were frozen in their tracks, too scared to move quickly. It all happened too fast.

He spat a nasty word at them, and by then Chip was finally moving, half jumping and half falling out of his way. But not so Benny. Chip had a confused picture of the man's hand poking Benny in the face, and heard his brother scream with pain, and then the man was past them, running up a side street.

Chip scrambled over to Benny, who had fallen backward into the snow with his hands on his face.

"What's the matter, Benny?" he cried, but Benny could only scream. Chip turned his head toward the bus, looking for help from Mr. Fader. He was in time to see the driver lurch toward the open door, gasping, and then stumble down the steps and fall to his knees in the snow. Down at the grocery store, someone stuck his head out of the door. Slowly Mr. Fader struggled to his feet and staggered toward the store.

"Help!" yelled Chip. "Help!"

"My face!" Benny shrieked in his ear. Chip pried Benny's hand away from his cheek and looked. He could see an ugly, raised mark on it that made him want to vomit. The cigarette! The man had jammed his cigarette in Benny's face.

Chip grabbed a handful of snow and pressed it against Benny's cheek, and that was the right idea. Benny gasped, and stopped screaming.

"That help?"

"Yes!"

"You hold it!"

People were coming out of the store now, helping Mr. Fader inside. The door closed behind them. The boys were alone in the snow. Chip looked the other way, with a wild rage burning his insides, to see what had become of the man with the gun.

He was gone. The streets were peaceful and empty. Chip wanted to scream himself. Some punk had stuck a cigarette in his brother's face and got away, and there wasn't a thing he could do about it.

Then he saw something that changed his mind. Tracks in the snow.

"Benny, go home and let Mom take care of you. I'm going to follow his tracks and see where he goes!"

Benny pressed the snow hard against his face.

"I'm going with you."

"No!"

"Yes!"

The way Benny sounded made Chip stop, just as he was ready to insist. Benny was crying, but not whimpering. Benny was mad! Besides, there wasn't time to argue. The way it was snowing, there was not a minute to lose.

"It doesn't hurt, honest, Chip!"

"Okay, come on!"

So stumbling through the snow, with Benny pressing a handful of it against his cheek, they hurried as fast as they could up the side street. The tracks were already beginning to fill in. At least that meant the man wasn't very close. Or did it? If he stopped and hid somewhere, the tracks would keep on filling in, while he waited. . . . Blinking and shaking snowflakes out of his eyes, Chip peered ahead, frightened at the thought of actually seeing a tall figure loom up in front of them, yet unwilling to turn back and just let him go.

On both sides of the street there were only dark, silent houses, or dull patches of light behind drawn shades. The houses were small and shabby, jammed together with hardly any space between them. Beat-up trash cans were sitting in a crooked row on the sidewalks, waiting for a city truck to come around that probably wouldn't make it that night. Every black space between the houses made his heart beat faster, made him won-

der what he would do if suddenly the tracks turned aside, and suddenly somebody stepped out of the shadows. . . .

But he kept his eyes on the tracks, and Benny kept the snow against his face and only groaned now and then, and they trudged on through drifts that were beginning to make it hard to tell where they were. In the swirl of snow that spun around them like a cold beaded curtain, nothing looked familiar. But the tracks kept going, and the boys kept going. And at last the tracks took a sudden turn to the right, toward Milford Avenue.

When they reached the avenue, that was the end of them. They disappeared into a crisscross of other tracks on that busy thoroughfare, where even in a snowstorm there were people coming and going. Chip looked up at the street sign.

Keaney Street.

They were not far from their school. Every morning they walked past this corner on their way up the avenue. But Keaney Street was forbidden territory. Keaney Street was one of the toughest sections in their end of town. Three people kept them out of it: their father, their mother, and Marty Rennick. Keaney Street was Marty's territory.

The question was, had the man with the gun crossed the avenue, or not?

2

LOGIC, his father always said. "You got to use logic. And not just any old logic, either. You got to put your-self in the other guy's shoes and use *his* logic. Because your logic may not be his logic."

Chip was not sure he understood all that, but he did understand the part about putting himself in the other guy's shoes. That man, now. Why had he turned off a quiet side street, where nobody was outside and practi-cally every house had its lights off or its shades pulled, and walked over to a main street where even in a snow-storm there were people around? Chip could think of only two reasons why. Either he lived on Milford Ave-nue, or he had to cross it to get home. Home or wher-ever he was going, but on a night like this wouldn't even a crook head for home?

"I'll bet he crossed the street," said Chip. "I'll bet he went down Keaney Street."

Benny stared across and shuffled his feet uneasily.

"Keaney Street! Gee, you want to go there, Chip?"

"Well . . . let's cross over and see if any tracks go that way."

They waited while a snowplow and an emergency truck passed, then hurried over the broad avenue and stood on the corner, looking down the narrow street that stretched ahead of them, silent, dark, and uninviting.

"What if Marty Rennick and his guys are out?"

"Aw, I bet they won't be." Chip tried to sound surer than he felt. "Come on, we'll just go a little way."

As nervous as two rabbits, looking in every direction between hasty glances at the snow, they set foot in Keaney Street for the first time in their lives. For a few steps there was dim light shining through the cluttered windows of the corner store to give them courage, but when they left the windows behind there was only a long stretch of blank brick wall beside them, all the way to the back end of the store. Halfway down the block, only a week ago, a man had been knifed, but Chip tried not to think about that.

The snow on the corner had been well trampled, but now the tracks thinned out. Not enough, though. There was still not just one set ahead, but several. Still, there were some that seemed spaced apart just about the right distance. Chip stretched his stride to match them and measure them.

A snowball missed them by inches and exploded with a click against the wall.

"Come on, Benny!" cried Chip. They got out of there fast, back to the corner, while another snowball whizzed by and hit a parking sign so close it sprayed snow down on them.

"Hold it — Okay, let's go!" said Chip, after a quick

glance in both directions had showed the street clear of traffic. Back of them they heard a whoop of jeering laughter. They darted across Milford Avenue and kept up a stumbling run through the snow as best they could, back the way they had come. They could have gone home down the avenue, but they didn't stop to think about that. Across the avenue was out of Marty's territory, and straight ahead was still farther out, and that was the place to be. The side street across from Keaney even had a different name.

When Chip had time to look back, he was glad to see nobody was following them.

"Whew! I wonder who that was? Did you hear those snowballs hit? Their snowballs have rocks in them."

He might have relaxed, except that now a new worry started gnawing at him.

"We got to get home. Mom will be crawling up the wall!"

"Well, for once we've got a good excuse," said Benny, and scooped some fresh snow for his cheek.

"Yeah, but when she sees your face she'll really blow. How's it feel?"

"It's okay," mumbled Benny. "It was worse when I broke my leg. Gee, everything happens to me!"

"I should break my neck to make you feel better!"

"Good idea!" said Benny, and managed to laugh a little.

The wind was in their faces now, cold and bitter, and made them keep their heads down. They plodded through the drifts, following their own tracks home, theirs and the man's. Already these were no more than dents in the snow, filling in fast. Chip stretched his stride to match them and thought hard about the ones in Keaney Street. Yes, these felt just about the same as the ones he had measured there.

The side street was as silent as ever. On both sides there were houses full of people, and none of them knew that anything had happened. None of them knew a crumby punk with a gun in his pocket had come running up their street after trying to hold up Mr. Fader and

[17]

burning a little kid's face with a cigarette. Chip stared at the houses they were passing, and hated all the stupid people in them. Just for a minute he hated them. He wanted to throw snowballs through their windows and make them know something terrible had been going on outside while they sat in there paying no attention. But then the feeling passed, and he knew it was foolish. How many terrible things had happened in his own street that he never knew anything about until later? He could think of a few.

The wail of a siren broke through the snowy silence. It came from the direction of the avenue. They reached a corner in time to look over that way and see an ambulance pass, heading the same way they were going. Its red roof light turned and flashed, the siren blared and faded as the ambulance slid across the intersection and out of their sight.

"Say, I wonder how Mr. Fader is?" Chip exclaimed. "He looked bad. Maybe that's for him!"

"What happened to him?" asked Benny.

Chip told him. Benny had not even seen Mr. Fader stumble down off the bus. He had been in too much pain to notice anything else.

"Gee! Did that guy shoot him?"

"Of course not! There weren't any shots."

"Maybe he had a silencer on his gun."

"Aw, come on! I could see it, and it wasn't long enough to have a silencer on it."

"Okay, okay. Then why did Mr. Fader fall off the bus?"

"Don't ask me. He looked scared stiff, is all I know. We'll find out."

"I hope they catch that bum!" said Benny, and called him a couple of things that Chip would have given him the back of his hand for saying at any other time. But now, of course, he had to make allowances.

"Boy, I hate to think what Mom would do if she heard you say words like that," said Chip.

"Well, that's what he is!"

"I know, but take it easy. Listen, did you get a good look at him?"

"Well, sort of."

"What did his face look like?"

Benny shivered, but not from the cold.

"It was crazy! He had a crazy smile, and big front teeth sticking down —"

"He had a mask on!" A thrill went through Chip as suddenly he realized that was the answer to the night-marish face they had seen. "He had a mask on! That face wasn't *real*. That was some kooky kind of mask, and that's why he looked so crazy!"

"Maybe you're right."

" 'Course I'm right! Did you think that was his real face, for Pete's sake?" snorted Chip, forgetting he had just figured it out himself. "What else did you see? What was he wearing?"

"How should I know?"

"Come on, *think* about it! *I* can remember!"

"Well . . ."

"Did he have on an overcoat?"

"No. He had on a jacket."

"That's right. It was a kind of light brown, tan-colored jacket, and it hit him — well, about here," said Chip, holding his hand at the level of his hip. "He had the collar turned up, and it had fur on it, around his face."

"And he had a belt with a big buckle!" said Benny, remembering something that had been at eye level for him. "A big square buckle, sort of yellow."

"Like brass?"

"Yeah, like brass. His jacket lifted a little, and I saw it when he was coming at us."

"Good! You remember that," said Chip earnestly. "Don't forget it."

"I won't."

"What about his pants?"

"They were dark colored."

"That's right. Anything else?"

Benny thought hard.

"No."

"He had some kind of black boots on," said Chip. "They went right by me. I'm lucky he didn't stomp me. He's the kind that would if he thought of it. So we've got a jacket with a fur collar turned up, and a big square brass belt buckle, and black boots."

Now Benny caught on, and he had to jeer.

"Who do you think you are — Pop?"

"Shut up," snapped Chip. He knew he was imitating his father, but it annoyed him to have his little squirt of a brother get funny about it. His father was like a detective already, the way he thought things out, and as soon as he got promoted he would *be* a detective, instead of riding around in a prowl car with Patrolman Rooney.

"Wait'll Pop hears about me," said Benny fiercely. *"He'll* fix that monkey!"

Monkey. That was their father's favorite word for a small-time thug. The big-time ones were apes.

"Got to find him first," Chip pointed out, and felt a sag of discouragement at the thought. They still didn't have much to go on. Guys dressed like him were a dime a dozen, and they hadn't seen his real face at all. Over around Milford Avenue and Keaney Street you could find two or three on any corner any time, except when the weather was like now.

At last there were a few extra twinkles ahead, shining through the snowfall when it didn't blot them out, and soon they were back in Stedman Square. As they came nearer, they could see a police car pulling away from in front of the store.

"Hey, look!"

"I'll bet it was Perelli and Muldoon!"

"Maybe. Gee, if Pop happened to be with them, catching a ride home! . . ."

"Yeah, maybe. Look, here's where the guy burned me!"

There were still big dents in the snow where they had fallen. Nobody had walked over them yet.

"Him and his dirty cigarette!" Chip said angrily — and it was lucky he did. Because talking about the cigarette gave him an idea.

"Stop!"

Benny was about to step on the dent where he had fallen. Chip grabbed him and dragged him back by the arm so hard he made Benny drop his handful of snow.

"Hey, what —"

"Maybe we can find that cigarette! It's got his fingerprints on it! Remember, he didn't have any gloves on?"

"I guess so." Benny scooped a new handful of snow for his cheek. "But it's all covered up by now. How are you going to find a white cigarette in a bunch of snow?"

"We can try. It must have dropped close to where you fell. And one end will be black, so maybe . . . Now, I got to be careful . . ."

Kneeling on the near side of the dent where Benny had fallen, Chip started to reach across it. Just in time he remembered his knitted gloves. Their mother always made them carry gloves or mittens and tried to make them wear them, but they seldom got around to it. This time it was a good thing they hadn't. As he said to Benny when he pulled them out of his pocket now, "Well, at least they're dry."

"You almost forgot them," Benny had to point out, like a typical kid brother.

"Oh, drop dead," suggested Chip. With his left hand he began to comb away the top layer of snow while Benny watched over his shoulder. And as luck would have it, Benny saw it even before he did.

"There it is!"

Chip almost made a grab for it. He caught himself just in time, and remembered to hold up his right hand for Benny to admire. "See? I saved a dry glove to pick it up with!"

"You're lucky I saw it!"

"*I* saw it!" growled Chip. "Just because I didn't yell the very second . . ."

With the greatest of care he picked the cigarette out of the snow. It was crumpled into a split and crooked butt from being jammed into Benny's face.

"How do we know it's his?" asked Benny.

With his free hand Chip slapped himself on the forehead and rolled his eyes up.

"How do we know it's his!" he groaned. "Who else has been standing around here in a snowstorm smoking cigarettes?"

"Okay, okay. It's probably his," Benny decided.

Being careful not to crush it, Chip wrapped his hand finger by finger around the precious butt, cradling it in his palm.

"Let's go. I got to get this home!"

"What about the store? Aren't you going to stop at the store?"

"No! This is more important."

"What about Pop's cream?"

"Listen, when he sees you, he won't need any cream for his coffee, he'll need a drink!"

Still, Benny had a point. They were there, they might as well get the cream. Besides, that's what they had been sent out for in the first place.

"Oh, all right, we'll stop at the store. The money's in my right pocket. Reach in and get it."

"Okay."

"It's fifty cents."

"I know. I saw Mom give it to you."

Benny reached in and fished out the fifty-cent piece. And of course he dropped it in the snow.

"For crying out loud, can't you do anything right?" cried Chip, as Benny went to his knees and pawed around for the coin with his free hand. Then all at once Chip stopped being mad and started laughing like a crazy man. "Yikes, we're really something! You got one hand, and *I* got one hand!"

Then Benny started laughing, and the two of them were doubled up when old Mrs. Flanahan came out of the store on her way home. Old Mrs. Flanahan always found fault with everything. She gave them a look and a sniff.

"A fine time to be skylarking, when poor Mr. Fader's been took to the hospital with a heart attack after being held up!" she snapped, and crunched away through the snow. The boys stopped laughing and stared at each other.

"A heart attack!"

"That ambulance *was* for him!"

They thought about Mr. Fader, going back up the avenue he had driven his bus along a thousand times, and then Chip said, "Well, come on, let's find the money and get going."

They located the coin, and Chip took charge of it. He started to pull the door open, and Benny was right behind him. Chip stopped and looked over his shoulder, causing a collision.

"Where do you think you're going?"

"With you!"

"Oh, boy! You go inside holding that snow on your face, and everybody will want to know why. And we haven't got time for that. You wait out here!"

Chip slipped inside. Several people were there, all talking excitedly. He told Mr. Kasmelian what he wanted, and the grocer put a carton of cream in a small paper bag without once really looking at him. He was busy telling another customer what had happened.

While he was still talking he took Chip's fifty cents, rang up the sale, and made change. Chip counted the change and worked it awkwardly into his pocket with his left hand. While he was at it, somebody noticed him and remembered he was a cop's kid.

"Hey, tell your old man some bum tried to stick up Fader the bus driver and now he's in the hospital!"

"Fader, not the bum," said someone else.

"And what are the cops going to do about it?"

"Nothing, probably. They never do. What do we pay taxes for?"

"I'll tell him," said Chip, his hand firm around the cigarette butt.

"Lot of good that'll do! It's getting so nobody's safe on the streets any more . . ."

Chip slipped out of the door and jerked his head at Benny.

"Come on, let's go. Bunch of bigmouths!"

"What's the matter?"

"Aw, nothing."

It wasn't always easy, being a cop's kid.

3

THERE WERE fresh tire tracks in their street now, and footsteps going up in front of their house.

"Look, I'll bet Pop's home."

"Somebody gave him a lift."

The Bradys' car was at a garage being fixed. The boys toiled up the slope and followed their father's footsteps around the side of the house, both stretching their strides so as to step in them. It was all Benny could do to make it. As they started up the outside back stairs, Chip said, "If Pop comes to the door, be ready to duck."

"Talk fast," said Benny.

Before they even got to the top of the stairs, the door opened.

"That you?"

"Yes, Pop."

"You get up here! Your mother —"

"Something happened, Pop! It wasn't our fault!"

"That's what you always say. Come on, get up here!"

"We saw a guy try to stick up Fader the bus driver and we yelled and he ran and we followed him and — and that's not all!" said Chip, spitting it all out in a hurry before coming within range of his father's swing.

Sergeant Brady's wrath faded satisfactorily into a jaw-dropping look of astonishment. He was a big man

with a ruddy complexion and jet black hair, and his jaw was a heavy, solid one. He was still in his dark blue uniform, but he had taken off the heavy belt and holster that held his service revolver.

"What's all this?" he asked, still frowning. But he stood aside to let them come in, and they did not have to duck. Behind him their mother was making various sounds having to do with relief, fear, and concern. They entered in a spray of snowflakes and then remembered their boots.

"That's all right, I'll have to mop the floor anyway," said Mrs. Brady. "Take your things off and . . ."

She paused to stare as Chip carefully laid the cigarette butt on the kitchen table.

"Chip Brady! What is *that?*"

"Don't touch it, Mom! It's a clue!"

"A what?" She glanced wide-eyed at their father and at Benny, and then took a second look at Benny. "And why are you holding your cheek?"

The boys exchanged a "here we go!" glance.

"He's okay, Mom."

"Sure I am, Mom!"

"Let me see!"

She pulled Benny's hand away, and his handful of snow splattered on the kitchen floor. His wet cheek was not a pretty sight. It brought something between a gasp and a scream from their mother.

"Benny! What happened to you?"

"Aw, the guy stuck his cigarette in my face!"

"He *what?*"

"Who did?" thundered their father. His dark eyes were blazing, and his mouth had thinned to a tight line. Mrs. Brady seized Benny's arms, stared in horror at his cheek, then crumpled into a chair and burst into tears.

"Oh! He'll be marked for life!"

Grimly their father was disciplining his temper, bringing it under control, as any good policeman had to learn to do, quickly and effectively. He stooped and inspected Benny's burn with the eye of an expert.

"Hmm . . . maybe not. It looks bad, but I don't think it goes deep. Benny must have jerked away the instant it touched him, and . . . Now, now, dear, don't get yourself hysterical."

He calmed their mother down enough to take a second look, and that calmed her down still more. She had to admit it; ugly as it was, it didn't seem to be a deep burn.

Sergeant Brady helped Benny out of his padded jacket. Then he pulled a chair sideways from the table and sat down.

"Now, begin at the beginning, boys. Chip, what happened?"

Chip told the story in detail, from the start. Mrs. Brady flew off to the medicine cabinet, and while they talked she put something on Benny's burn and stuck a bandage over it. Benny interrupted when it came time to tell about how the man burned him, but Chip couldn't blame him for that. After all, it was his burn.

Their father stayed calm while they told their story, but anger still showed in his face. When Chip told how they had followed the man, however, the policeman's eyes flashed in a different way. And when Chip got to the part about looking for the cigarette, and remembering to pick it up with his glove on, a little smile began to twitch at the corners of his father's mouth.

"Runs in the family," he muttered, with a quick glance at his wife. Then his eyes came back intently to Chip. "Sure you got the right butt?"

"Yes! It was only covered by about an inch of snow. An old one would have been way underneath. So this one's got to be it."

"When he was still on the bus, you could see the gun in his hand. Was it the hand nearest you?"

Chip thought about it, and nodded.

"Yes."

"That would be his right hand, then. Did he still have the gun in his hand when he came at you?"

"Yes. I know, because I remember, now, he sort of swung it at me. I saw it shine."

"You're sure he didn't have gloves on?"

"Yes, sir! Huh, Benny?"

"That's right!"

Sergeant Brady nodded thoughtfully.

"Makes sense, of course. You don't wear gloves if you can help it when you want to handle a gun."

He stared at the cigarette butt.

"Run get me an envelope out of the desk drawer, Chip."

Chip hurried down the hall, went to the desk in a corner of the small, plainly furnished living room, and found an envelope. When he brought it back, his father scooped the butt into it with a spoon (which his mother seized and took to the sink for immediate washing) and sealed the envelope.

"I'll send this down to Galton in Fingerprints first thing in the morning. He may be able to lift some prints from it."

But he looked gloomy as he laid the envelope aside. Sitting with his legs planted apart, he drove his big fist into the palm of his left hand, a picture of frustration.

"Why did this have to happen just now? Any other time I'd make them turn me loose to find that monkey myself, but I'm down for a special detail tomorrow, and I'm walking a tightrope as it is, with this promotion hanging fire. The Commissioner's the kind that calls it a sign of weakness if you give a thought to your own family or anything else personal. Not that I'll probably get the nod anyway, now that it's between Bresnahan and me. Not with his connections."

He jumped to his feet and made the kitchen floor shake with his stride.

"What next? The car's transmission is shot, it'll cost a fortune to fix. Bresnahan's probably going to give me the elbow. And now some small-time thug burns a hole in my kid's face. My own son! What a dirty business it is!" he said, sagging down into his chair again.

Pain stabbed through Chip at the sight of him, for his father looked almost defeated, and that was a look he seldom had. Usually, no matter what happened, he would get a hard grin on his face, and turn his thumbs up and say, "Well, you can't keep a good man down!" But right now he looked like a beat-up prizefighter sitting in his corner wondering if he could come out for the next round.

"But, gee, Pop, if they get his fingerprints they'll find him, won't they?"

Sergeant Brady frowned.

"They won't get too much off a cigarette. Part of a thumb and part of a forefinger, maybe. And even then you can't count on anything. He may not have a police record yet, a punk like that, sticking up a bus driver to get a few bucks. He was young, wasn't he?"

"Well, he ran like a young guy."

"Sure." Sergeant Brady sighed wearily. "Oh, it stinks, it stinks! We don't even get all the murderers, or the ones that pull the big jobs, let alone the small fry. Do you know how many calls we get as serious as this one?

A dozen a day, sometimes. And there's only so many of us to check them out — not enough of us by any means. Oh, the boys will try a little harder on this one, when they hear about Benny, but in the meantime they got to be thinking about a dozen other cases — the Balachi murder, the Gorham Company robbery, and plenty more."

U. S. 1442265

For a moment he sat with his shoulders sloping and his hands hanging limp. But then he stirred himself, cleared his throat, and pulled out his notebook.

"Still, we can hope. Now, I want you to describe that monkey for me again. Give me everything you know. I'm going to write it up to turn in tomorrow."

This was more like it. The boys stood beside him at the table, and for a while they were busy, telling him everything they could remember.

"Tan jacket . . . fur-lined collar turned up . . . dark pants . . . big square brass belt buckle — that's good, Benny . . . black boots . . . What did he have on his head?"

"Oh!" Chip was mad at himself for having forgotten all about that. He thought hard. "Some kind of cap."

"Cloth? Wool?"

"Fuzzy. Wool, I guess. I think it was dark green."

"Brown," said Benny.

"Okay, green or brown, probably wool. Long bill? Short bill?"

"In between."

"Hair. Did you notice what color it was?"

They exchanged a glance, and shook their heads.

"All right. Now, this mask. Black?"

"No, sort of skin-colored, almost, but with red cheeks."

"Did it cover his eyes?"

"No, I don't think so. It was between his eyes and his mouth. It was a really crazy kind of mask, with those two goofy teeth and all. It didn't go around his eyes. It started below them. It had an upper lip, with those two big teeth hanging down from the middle of it, and big cheeks. Made him have a real kooky face. I'd sure know it if I saw that mask again!"

"Well, I don't expect he'll be running around wearing it any more, and you'll never recognize him without it. For that matter, eyewitnesses aren't as good as people like to think, anyway. Plenty of times they can't pick out the man they saw, even when they're sure they can. Often as not an eyewitness is the poorest witness you can put on the stand at a trial."

Even so, there was a touch of pride in their father's eyes as he closed his notebook and looked at them.

"That's a pretty good description, though, for a couple of kids. It's a whole lot better than nothing. Now I'll get on the phone and call in to see what they know at the station, and see if I can find out how Fader's doing. I wonder who took the report at the store?"

"We didn't get there in time to see," said Chip, "but maybe it was Sergeant Perelli."

"Could be. Well, we'll find out."

"And while your father's on the phone I want you two to get ready for bed."

Somehow the word "bed" made Benny think of his cheek. He groaned and held his hand over it tenderly.

"Aw, Mom, I can't get to sleep yet with my cheek hurting me!"

His mother gave him a sharp glance that was not without a glint of motherly humor. Benny had not been showing many signs of pain in the last few minutes, until now.

"Does it still hurt so much? Maybe we'd better call the doctor."

"I don't want any doctor!" cried Benny, alarmed.

"Well, then, let's you get ready for bed, and I'll bet you'll be able to go to sleep if you really try."

"I've still got that problem to do," Chip reminded her.

"You can stay up a few minutes longer, but I want you in bed soon, too."

At the telephone beside the hall door, their father paused in the midst of dialing his number and glanced over his shoulder.

"Maybe a little something to eat first would help," he said, bringing quick grins to his sons' faces. Their mother looked from one of them to the other.

"Three men against one woman. It isn't fair. All right, you may have something before you go to bed — but only if you get ready first!"

The news about Mr. Fader was not good. His heart attack was a serious one, and he was being kept absolutely quiet.

"He probably won't be able to add much to what you two remembered, even when he can talk," said their father, while they sat at the table with him enjoying cake and milk. "The only thing is, it might help to know where that monkey got on the bus, and Fader should be able to remember. Not many people out tonight. The one thing you can usually count on, as far as this kind of punk is concerned, is that he's stupid. If you can't think of anything better to do than stick up a bus driver, you have to be stupid. So there's a good chance he got on the bus near where he lives. The way a monkey like that works is, he starts out with the idea he's going to stick up somebody. He's got a gun and a mask. But he doesn't have a plan, he's just looking around. So he sees a bus coming along with only a couple of passengers or maybe nobody on it, and he gets an idea. He'll hop on and ride to the end of the line and then put on his mask and stick up the bus driver. Now I ask you, does that sound like an intelligent idea?"

"He sounds like a dope to me," said Chip.

"He *is* a dope. But a dangerous dope, because he's

mean and nasty, and he'll just as likely pull the trigger as not. You were right to yell, but still it's a lucky thing he didn't lose his head and plug Fader — or one of you when he jumped off," added Sergeant Brady, with his face going a little gray at the thought. "A jerk that stops to light a cigarette first — he's got a picture of himself in his twisted little mind, looking tough and cool, like some actor he saw on TV. I tell you, his kind are like a stick of dynamite with a short fuse. Anything can happen. And I thank the good Lord that more didn't. Well, now, off to bed, Benny, and you get to work, Chip, and we'll see what we can do about this in the morning."

Chip looked across the table at his father for a moment, and while their eyes met he could feel himself growing older with a sudden rush. For the first time he realized how, on that snowy evening, he and Benny had stared death in the face without knowing it.

4

THE FIRST THING next morning, Sergeant Brady turned on the radio to get the news. For that matter, he always did every morning. Usually Chip paid no attention to the news broadcast, but this time he listened eagerly. He and Benny even finished dressing in the kitchen to be close to the radio. They expected the broadcast to start right off with the story about the holdup attempt and Mr. Fader's heart attack. Instead there was a lot of stuff about Washington and Moscow and Vietnam, and something the President was doing, and then a commercial.

His father cocked his head at them with a crooked grin.

"You expected a special bulletin, maybe?" Already dressed and seated at the table, Sergeant Brady sipped his coffee. "Be lucky if they mention it at all. Besides, they start off with the national and international news. They haven't even got to the local news yet."

When the commercial ended and the newscaster began talking again, it was all about the snowstorm, and how many states it had covered, and how firemen had battled a blaze over on the North Side somewhere. Then, almost at the very end —

"During the snowstorm thieves broke into the Babson

Fur Shop on Taylor Avenue and made off with an estimated eight thousand dollars' worth of furs, and a bus driver suffered a heart attack in Stedman Square after a passenger attempted to hold him up and then fled when passersby shouted."

"Well! There you are!" Sergeant Brady saluted his sons mockingly. "Hello, passersby!"

"Is that all they're going to say?" Chip was indignant. It didn't seem like much, for something so important.

"You heard the fur robbery, eight thousand bucks' worth of furs, and that almost didn't make it, either. If it wasn't for Fader's heart attack they wouldn't even have bothered to mention a stickup attempt. You start paying attention to the news, and looking at the papers, Chip, and you'll see what I mean. Your story will be a couple of inches long on the third page."

He added more cream to his coffee and held up the carton, shaking his head thoughtfully as he looked at it.

"This is pretty special stuff, this cream. If it wasn't for this, you wouldn't have been out there last night. Maybe I ought to give it up!"

Mrs. Brady came into the kitchen tying an apron around her waist, and told Benny to keep his hands off the fresh bandage she had put on his cheek.

"Are you sure you feel all right?"

"Sure, Mom."

"He looks pale to me," she told their father, and felt Benny's forehead worriedly.

"Aw, I'm fine, Mom!"

"Well, just the same — Chip, I want you to check on him at lunchtime, and call me up from school."

"All right, Mom."

"For Pete's sake, you'd think I was dying, or something!"

"Pop, when will you know about the fingerprints?" asked Chip.

"Depends on how busy they are down there. When they get to it, they'll let me know. And then I'll let you know," said his father with a teasing grin. It was downright annoying, that grin.

The sky was clearing and the snow was melting. As
they walked to school up Milford Avenue, all the magic
and beauty of the night before was gone, lost in a gray
layer of dirty slush. The city was getting back to nor-
mal. The rasp of a dozen snow shovels on sidewalks
added their din to the rumble of traffic as men shoved
slush toward the curb in front of barbershops and fruit
stands, drugstores and meat markets, thrift shops and
delicatessens, liquor stores and newsstands. Milford
Avenue was never exactly a beauty spot of the nation,
and it looked worse than usual now. But the boys were

used to it, and never gave it a thought. Besides, they both had other things on their minds.

"Wait till the other kids hear what happened to *me!*" said Benny. He was looking forward to being the center of attention.

"How's your cheek feel now?"

"Aw, it doesn't hurt hardly at all!" said Benny, feeling his bandage.

"Keep your dirty mitts off that," said Chip sternly. "You know what Mom said."

"Okay, okay."

"You're lucky he didn't stick that butt in your eye, the dirty rat," said Chip. "Listen, I been thinking. If that monkey does live around Keaney Street, we might see him along here any time, so we got to keep our eyes open. We got to keep looking for black boots and a brass belt buckle, especially that buckle."

"Pop said I was pretty good, seeing that," Benny reminded him proudly.

"Sure, you're a regular Sherlock Holmes. But keep looking. Every time we walk back and forth, we got to watch, because nobody knows better than we do what he looked like."

"And *we* don't know too much."

When they reached the corner of Keaney Street, Chip paused to stare down it for a moment. It made his skin crawl, just to look. Was their monkey down that street somewhere, maybe sleeping in some back room upstairs in one of those ramshackle houses, with his kooky mask hidden in a drawer and his gun under a floorboard in the closet, like the one Pop told about finding once?

"If he does live down there, this is one corner I bet he hangs out on," Chip muttered. He glanced all around, and made a contemptuous face. "A bum like that wouldn't be up yet, but when we come home this afternoon we'll keep our eyes peeled."

Chip got quite a bit of attention from his classmates when he told his story. Of course, he was very offhanded and cool about it, especially when the girls were listening. Even his homeroom teacher, Mrs. French, asked him what had happened, and he had to go through the whole story for her. But all this was nothing compared to Benny's day. Chip got permission to go speak to him at lunchtime, and when he saw him Chip almost had to laugh. Benny was so flushed and excited that it was a good thing their mother couldn't see him, or she would have started feeling his forehead again.

"Mrs. Wheatley let me stand up and tell the whole class all about what happened!" he announced importantly. Chip knew it was a waste of time to ask him how he felt. Benny was feeling great. But he went through the motions anyway.

"You feel okay?"

"Sure!"

"Okay, I'll call Mom and tell her."

He had permission to use the pay phone out in the

hall. He dropped in a dime and dialed his home number.

"Hello, Mom?"

"Hello, dear! Everything all right?"

"Sure, he's okay. He's the king of the fifth grade," growled Chip, and listened to his mother laugh. He told her everything Benny had said.

"How about you?"

"Oh, I told a couple of the guys," he said, trying to yawn a little. "And Mrs. French's ears were flapping, so I had to tell her, too."

"It must have been a strain," said his mother, with what sounded uncomfortably like a giggle. But then she made him feel good. "Your father phoned a few minutes ago. He knew you'd be calling, and he said to tell you they lifted a couple of good prints from your cigarette butt."

A tingle started somewhere around Chip's heels and zoomed up his spine deliciously.

"They did? Hey, that's super!"

"He said they haven't found any matching prints in the files so far," she added. "But maybe they will."

"I hope so! Thanks, Mom!"

"Thank your father. I'm just your messenger girl."

Chip said good-bye, and walked away on an air cushion. If any kid had made a smart crack about his father just then, even Marty Rennick, he would have flattened him with one punch, so help him!

When school was out, at three-fifteen, Chip collected Benny the glamour boy and started home.

"Okay, now, knock it off about how you wowed them in the fifth grade," ordered Chip, savoring the knowledge that he had a blockbuster up his own sleeve now. "Guess what Mom told me when I phoned her?"

"I don't know, what?"

Chip spilled it. To give Benny credit, he was impressed. But his response was not quite what Chip had expected.

"Boy!" said Benny. "My cigarette butt paid off after all!"

Chip was so outraged he stopped in his tracks.

"What do you mean, *your* cigarette butt? *I* found it!"

"Yes, but it burned *me!*"

Chip rolled up his eyes and took a deep breath.

"Man, if that's not the screwiest — Well, forget it. The big thing is, now we've really got to look for that monkey, see? Because if they could pick him up and take his prints, we'd really have him nailed, see?"

Benny saw.

"Okay, let's look."

They looked. The weather had improved considerably, becoming sunny and warm, and lots of people were out on the avenue as they walked home. Lots of people, including young guys in tan jackets all over the place, or so it seemed to them when they began to look around. But most of the men were the wrong size, or didn't have fur linings on their collars, or didn't look right some other way. When they came to a pool hall, Chip said, "Here's the kind of place he might be hanging out in," so they stopped and peered in through the door, which had a dingy square of plate glass in it. One man in a tan jacket was shooting pool, but when he straightened up and chalked his cue, Chip shook his head.

"Too short."

Then a man in a tan jacket with a fur-lined collar came out of a store a few doors down the street, but when he turned toward them they could see he had gray hair.

"Too old."

"Gee, we'll never find him," said Benny, discouraged. *"Everybody* wears those same jackets."

"Okay, but how many have you seen with black boots and a brass belt buckle so far?"

"None. But I can't even see their belt buckles, most of them."

"Well, you can see their feet, can't you? Watch for black boots."

They were halfway home when a man came swinging out of a barbershop and turned toward them. He was wearing a tan jacket with a fur collar, his boots were black, he was young and tall, and he was smoking a cigarette. His face was lean and hard. He looked tough.

They stopped short and goggled at him, and Benny said, "Hey! That could be him!" and Chip had presence of mind enough to say, "Yeah, well, stop looking at him! And duck your head down, so he won't see your bandage! Here, let's look in this window till he goes by!"

They turned and stared blindly into a window. As luck would have it, they were in front of an empty store, and there was nothing in the window but a tattered poster advertising a dance, a firemen's ball that had been held two months ago. The black boots clicked toward them on the sidewalk, and Chip's eyes began to focus on the reflection in the window of the dark store. He could see the street behind him. He watched the man pass, and saw his glance flick their way for an instant as he went by. Then their heads turned to watch him as he strode on up the street.

"What'll we do now, Chip?"

"Did you watch him in the window?"

"Yes."

"Could you see his belt buckle?"

"No, could you?"

"No."

"How about running ahead of him and trying again?"

"You crazy? No, I got a better idea. Let's follow him till he throws away his cigarette! If we can only get that, we'll really have something."

"Huh?"

"Don't you see? If they could compare the fingerprints on it with the ones on ours, then they'd *know* if it's him! So we follow him, and grab his cigarette when he throws it away, and see where he goes."

Clutching their schoolbooks tightly in their excitement, they turned and began to trail their suspect back up the avenue. At the corner he turned off and went down a side street.

"Now what?" said Benny.

Chip took a deep breath. It wasn't Keaney Street, but it was only a couple of blocks this side.

"We follow him. We've got just as much right to walk that way as he has."

"Maybe he recognized us!"

"We've got to take that chance. Anyway, I'll bet he didn't. He wasn't acting nervous, or anything."

"Maybe he'll wonder why we turned around and came back."

"We've got to take that chance, too."

They turned the corner, and saw their man still ahead of them, strolling along unhurriedly, still smoking his cigarette.

But then he turned again and disappeared between two buildings.

The boys gave each other a flustered glance, and hurried ahead, until they reached the point where he had disappeared. It was nothing more than an alley, narrow and rubbish strewn, running between the store buildings on Milford Avenue and a factory on the next street.

Edging forward, they took a cautious look around the corner of the store building at the end of the alley. Their suspect had walked almost to a point where the blank sidewall of a store building cut all the way across the passage, making it a blind alley. When they looked, he was doing the very thing Chip had hoped for. He was flipping away his cigarette. Then he turned toward the back end of a store, and disappeared once more.

They stared down the length of the alley, which looked as dark and gloomy as an abandoned tunnel. The distance between them and the cigarette butt smoldering on a pile of unmelted, soot-speckled snow in that narrow alley seemed enormous. But there was no stopping now, and anyway, their suspect had gone inside somewhere. With a rush that gave them courage they ran into the alley. If they could only run in, grab the butt, and run out again fast enough, they would be able to do it without losing their nerve.

"Hey, I got to put on my gloves!" Chip remembered. "Here, hold my books, Benny."

He loaded up the smaller boy to the level of his chin, then darted forward, eager to grab the prize and leave that ugly, frightening alley behind.

"What's going on?"

A hard voice turned him into jelly. He looked around to find their suspect standing over him, hard-eyed and tight-lipped.

"What do you kids think you're doing? Why are you tailing me?"

Chip's head swam, his mind was a blank. He could think of nothing to do but point to the cigarette.

"I wanted your butt!"

The truth happened to be the best approach, in an unexpected way. The sharp face changed.

"You what? How old are you?"

"Twelve."

"Twelve? Listen, I didn't start smoking till I was nearly fourteen — and now I wish I hadn't. In fact, I'm thinking of giving it up. You want to ruin your lungs, you little jerk?"

Scornfully their suspect stamped his heel on the smoldering butt.

"Now beat it, before I knock your heads together! And don't go around picking up any more butts, you hear?"

Chip and Benny did not need a second invitation. They were on their way immediately. But Benny was overloaded. He hadn't gone ten feet before he was dropping books in all directions. Chip had to stop and scoop them up. Behind him he could hear their suspect chuckling.

Even so, they didn't slow down until they were back on Milford Avenue. By that time they were so badly winded they had to stop and catch their breath.

"*Now* what?" gasped Benny, once he had gulped enough air to be able to talk.

"I don't know," snapped Chip, brushing dirt and snow off his books.

"At least we know where he went."

"Oh, for Pete's sake, he's not our monkey!" Chip said disgustedly.

"What makes you so sure?"

"Listen, did he act like a guy who'd shove a cigarette in your face?"

"Well . . . no."

"Okay, then! Let's go home!"

Tan jackets! Black boots! When half the guys in town went around wearing them, how was a fellow supposed to pick out one special monkey from the bunch of them?

5

THEY WALKED down Milford Avenue again, past the empty store with the poster for the firemen's ball, past the barbershop the man had come out of. Benny was enjoying the thought of having still another story to tell.

"Wait till Pop hears about *this!*"

The remark brought a big-brother groan from Chip.

"What? Listen, we've got to keep quiet about this, you hear? If Mom thought we were running into alleys, trying to tail somebody, she'd go right off the launch pad! Why, she'd probably start coming to school to walk us home herself!" said Chip, and the picture of that was enough to make him shudder.

Benny was disappointed.

"You mean we can't even tell Pop?"

"You know he doesn't keep secrets from Mom. Besides, he'd probably get worried, too."

Benny sighed, and made the sacrifice.

"Okay, I won't say anything, then."

He walked along in silence for a moment, and his excitement faded into discouragement.

"Heck, what's the difference, anyway?" he grumbled. "I don't see how we're ever going to find that monkey."

Having Benny take this attitude helped Chip to resist it.

"We're going to keep looking, that's how," he declared. "I wish I was invisible. I'd go into Keaney Street and hang around till I spotted him."

"Yeah, and then grab him from behind and scare him to death," said Benny, building up the story. "I'd like to be an invisible man and grab him and go 'Ooooooooooh!' right in his ear!"

Chip was busy with a new line of thought.

"Well, if we can't go into Keaney Street, we can do the next best thing," he said presently. "Listen, when we get home, I'm going to get out Pop's big street map, and lay out a plan."

"What do you mean?"

"You'll see. Come on, let's hurry. Mom will be waiting for us, to find out how you feel," Chip predicted, and he was right. When they came in, the first thing she did was feel Benny's forehead. And she had all the stuff ready to make a fresh bandage with.

Of course, Benny had to tell her the whole story of his big day at school. By now, anyone would have thought the burn was some kind of prize he had won. Chip stood it as long as he could, and then put in a few words of his own.

"You should have seen Mrs. French. I had her tongue hanging out when I told her about everything, she was so excited."

"I'm sorry I wasn't there," said Mrs. Brady. "I'd love to see Mrs. French with her tongue hanging out, not to mention her ears flapping."

Her twinkling eyes sawed Chip down to a sheepish grin.

"Well, anyway, she was excited."

"I'm sure she was. Now, let's have a look at the famous burn, and change the bandage."

Mrs. Brady carefully loosened the adhesive tape that held the bandage in place, and pulled it away. She was pleased with what she saw.

"I must say, you boys seem to heal overnight. That's really coming along very nicely. I don't think you'll even have a scar."

Benny greeted this unpleasant news with the dismay it deserved.

"No scar?" he cried worriedly.

"I should hope not! You certainly wouldn't want a scar, would you, silly?"

"Well, not a big one," Benny admitted, "but just a little one wouldn't hurt any."

Chip hooted.

"Oh, boy! This nut ought to be in one of those African tribes we read about, that make scars all over their faces!" he said, pretending to be scornful. But actually, of course, he could understand Benny's feelings.

"Well, there won't be any scar if *I* have anything to do with it," said Mrs. Brady sternly, "and you just put any such ridiculous notions out of your head, young man. The very idea!"

She put a fresh bandage on Benny's cheek, gave the boys some milk and cookies, and then slipped on her coat.

"I'm going over to see Mrs. Walters for a minute," she said. Mrs. Walters was an elderly neighbor who was ill. "Your father will be home early tonight, so why don't you get your work done, so that we can have some fun after supper?"

"We will," said Chip.

But first, however, before they settled down to their homework, he had his plan to think of. As soon as their mother had left, he said, "Let's look at the map."

He went to the desk in the living room and took the big street guide out of a drawer. Unfolding the map, he spread it on the floor, then got down on his hands and knees to study it. Benny was right beside him, of course, asking questions.

"What are you looking for?"

"Keaney Street. If we can't go into Keaney Street, we can do the next best thing. We can go all around it. I want to see how far it runs, and what streets are around it."

"Gee, this city is really big!" said Benny, surveying the map with civic pride. "Look at all the streets! Where's ours? Where's Hart Street?"

"Give me a minute, will you?"

At first the map was confusing. But then Chip saw some familiar names, and finally he located their neighborhood.

"Here's Stedman Square. And here's Hart Street, and our house is right . . . here!" he said, planting his finger triumphantly on the map.

"How about that?" said Benny. "And here's the park in the middle of the square, and here's where I got burned!"

"And there's Foley Street, where we chased that guy," said Chip. His finger moved into Stedman Square, took a left, and followed Foley Street until it reached the corner where they turned toward the avenue. "And over here is Milford Avenue. And here's Keaney Street!"

They stared curiously at the forbidden street. On the map it did not look particularly impressive. Just another small street leading off the broad avenue.

"One . . . two . . . three," said Chip running his finger along Keaney Street. "It's only three blocks long. That helps some."

"What does it run into at the other end?"

"Let's see. Beecher Avenue."

"Beecher Avenue?" They glanced at each other, and Benny shrugged. "I don't even remember what it looks like."

As is so often the way in a city, there were streets close to their own neighborhood that were completely unfamiliar to them. They had never had any reason to go over to Beecher Avenue. Perhaps they had ridden along it sometimes in the car, but if they had they paid no attention to where they were.

"Okay, Beecher Avenue. Now, let's see," said Chip. He drew a line of streets around Keaney Street with his forefinger. "Platt Street . . . Beecher Avenue . . . Fairmont Street . . . Milford Avenue. Those are the streets around Keaney. You know what we're going to do?"

"What?"

"We're going to walk home that way. Platt Street, Beecher Avenue, Fairmont Street. Especially Beecher Avenue, because he's likely to hang around on street corners on the big streets, where something is going on."

"Say, that's a good idea!" Benny admitted.

Chip was secretly pleased by Benny's approval. He was so pleased he dug Benny in the ribs with his elbow and then wrestled him joyously around on the living room floor for a couple of minutes, until he remembered the map.

"Hey, watch out for the map!"

Luckily they had rolled in the other direction. When they stopped wrestling, Chip sat up on one elbow and looked at the map again. Benny knelt beside it to look, too. Chip reached out and walked two fingers toward Keaney Street.

"Here I come, walking into Keaney," he said.

Benny walked two fingers into Keaney Street from the other direction. He lowered his voice to a growl.

"I'm Marty Rennick," he said. "Whatcha think you're doing in my territory?"

"Oh! Hi, Marty!" said Chip in a high, scared voice. "Why, gee whiz, Marty, I was just — er — I was just looking around."

"Yeh? Well, beat it, punk!" said Benny, and his fingers gave Chip's a couple of kicks.

"Hey, cut it out, you big bully!" whined Chip, and let Benny's fingers chase his halfway across town. They were enjoying this foolishness when suddenly they heard quick footsteps on the front porch.

"Hey! Here comes Mom!"

"Oh, boy! Let's get rid of this. I don't want to have to make excuses!"

Chip began hastily to fold up the map, so as to return it to its place. But haste makes waste, of course. It is one thing to unfold a large street map. It is another thing to fold it again. Chip tried about six different ways, but none of them worked. The air was full of map, flipping this way and that, but refusing to fold together.

"What's the matter, can't you fold it right?" asked Benny.

Chip paused to grit his teeth. If ever there was a typical kid-brother question this was it.

"No, I'm trying to fly it like a kite!" he snapped.

Now they could hear two voices downstairs.

"She's stopped to talk to Mrs. Harris."

"Good!"

"Hurry up!"

"I will, I will!"

Mrs. Harris was their downstairs neighbor. She was usually good for five minutes' conversation. Chip spread the map flat on the floor again. He glowered down at it angrily, and forced himself to slow down and think. That was what his father would do. "Never panic," his father said.

"Now, then," said Chip, trying to be deliberate. "We've got to figure this out one fold at a time. Let's see. First it goes this way . . ."

He was on the right track. The map began to come together.

"I've got it!"

But downstairs the meeting seemed to be breaking up. Mrs. Harris was not up to her usual five minute standard. Chip folded feverishly. The map surrendered. He jammed it back into the desk drawer. They raced on tiptoe down the hall to their room, and dived for their tables.

By the time the front door opened, their heads were bent over their books. But Chip was not thinking about algebra. He was thinking about Beecher Avenue.

After supper their father read aloud from a book

they were all enjoying. He had been reading from the same book, whenever they had the time, for a couple of weeks now. Sergeant Brady was a bug on good books, and education, and all that stuff. But he always chose books that had good stories, so that they had fun listening.

When he had finished reading, they talked about their monkey for a while.

"Sergeant Perelli will check out Keaney Street, don't you worry about that," said their father. "He knows it like the back of his hand. He knows everybody that lives there. But so far he can't think of anybody it might have been. Of course, there's one of the Rennick boys that's been in trouble pretty often, in fact I think he's in jail right now, but . . ."

"You mean, one of Marty Rennick's brothers, Pop?"

"That's right. There's about ten kids in that family, and they're all kinds. One of the boys is a priest, and one of the girls is a nun. Another boy is in Vietnam. Your cousin Fred was in the same outfit with him for a while, remember? But this kid you talk about, this Marty, well . . ."

Their father held his hand out flat, palm down, and rocked it from side to side.

"From what I hear, he could go either way. Stay away from him. He could be bad medicine."

6

PLATT STREET was the first street down from the school. When they turned into it next day, they felt the exciting lift that goes with beginning a new adventure. It was probably the only time Platt Street had ever looked exciting to anybody, and the excitement did not last long. Before they had gone a block, Platt Street had faded into what it was — a dull, drab, ordinary street. Its houses were small and plain, for the most part, and there were no stores. The only people in sight were a few old people, walking slowly along, picking their way around the last dirty patches of snow. A bakery truck went by, and one or two cars. A scruffy black-and-white dog barked at them from a porch.

At each corner Chip stared hungrily over toward Keaney Street, wishing he dared to go over there. Not that there seemed to be much more doing on Keaney. Nobody was in sight, not even any of the kids in Marty's gang.

"What a dead street!" complained Benny.

"Well, what did you expect? Wait'll we get to Beecher Avenue. That's our best bet, anyway," said Chip. When they reached the corner and turned into it, he said, "See? What did I tell you?"

But Benny was not impressed.

"Huh! Milford Avenue makes it look sick!"

Though Beecher Avenue was every bit as wide, it was obviously not as much of a shopping street. There were not as many markets and stores on it, and not as many people going in and out of them to give the street life and movement. Chip stopped on the corner for a look. Across the street was a lunch counter café, a tailor shop, and a barbershop. Next to the barbershop was a secondhand furniture store, and next to that a small movie theater, closed at that time of day. Red paint was peeling from its marquee. Under the marquee, the black doors and the shabby little box office could have used some fresh paint, too. Posters in grimy showcases advertised a Western. Beyond the movie theater was a cigar store, and then a bar. The bar was called the Beecher Tap.

A couple of men were eating at the lunch counter. A man was having his hair cut in the barbershop. A woman was sitting in a big overstuffed chair in the furniture store, reading a magazine. The window of the Beecher Tap had a curtain across its lower half, but they could see that there were several men inside, standing at the long bar. Except for a large woman in a bedraggled fur coat leading a big gray poodle whose coat was not much better, the sidewalk was empty. Nobody at all interesting was in sight.

Chip tried not to feel discouraged, but he could not help it. They would never find their man this way. It was asking too much to expect him to be standing around on a street corner at exactly the time of day they happened to come by. They needed to hang around for hours, watching people come and go, the way real detectives would have done. But they could not do that. They could not spend more than a few minutes looking around, because if they were too late getting home their mother would get worried. She would start asking a lot of questions.

For a moment Chip was ready to give up the whole business. It seemed hopeless. Of course, he knew what his father would have said. The one thing a detective had to have more than anything else was patience. Time and again he had said that. Patience. Chip wondered if he had enough. He knew that merely walking through his neighborhood once amounted to nothing at all. Only when they had walked home this way day after day for a couple of weeks — even a month! — would he have any right to give up. But the thought of trudging around the sides of Keaney Street day after day seemed about as dismal and boring as anything he could think of.

"Oh, well, one day at a time," he muttered, thinking out loud.

"What?"

"Nothing. Come on, let's see what's on this side of the street."

The first store they passed was a small variety store. Next to it was an electrical repair shop, and next to that a place that sold plumbing supplies. Beyond that was a grocery. An old lady came out of the grocery carrying a string shopping bag full of packages and turned into Keaney Street. She looked tough enough to be Marty Rennick's grandmother. On the corner a fat man was leaning against a lamppost, talking to another man they could not see. Then the fat man moved. The other man was leaning against a car parked at the curb. When they got a good look at him the boys stopped in their tracks.

"Chip!" said Benny, but before he could say anything more Chip grabbed his arm.

"Quiet! Take it easy!"

They were looking at black boots again, the right kind of black boots, on a young man the right size and height. Instead of a jacket with a fur collar, he had on a black leather one, and they could not see his belt buckle, but otherwise he looked just right.

"Pretend to look in the windows. We'll watch him for a while," said Chip. "He's busy talking, he's not paying any attention to us. Let's take a real good look at him."

"Okay, Chip. He could be our monkey, all right!"

They were standing in front of the electrical repair shop, keeping an eye on their suspect over their shoulders, when someone came out of the variety store. Chip glanced that way, and felt his mouth go dry.

It was the king of Keaney Street himself. Marty Rennick.

Marty was unwrapping a candy bar. He stared at them, and saw the bandage on Benny's cheek.

"Hey! Ain't you that kid that got burned in the stick-up at Stedman Square?"

Benny nodded rapidly. He knew it was Marty, too, and was too scared to speak. Big for his age, Marty seemed enormous close up, especially when he was giving somebody a hard look. His arrogant eyes turned to Chip, sending a chill down his spine.

"You his brother?"

"Yes."

"What are you guys doing over here?"

"Just walking home."

"Yeh? What are you walking this way for, if you live down at Stedman Square?"

Chip's mind went blank. He could not think of any reason to give that would fool a guy like Marty for one minute.

Then he thought, "Well, if I'm going to get belted for even being in his neighborhood, I might as well get belted for the real reason as for a phony one!" And at the same time, he thought of something that might work with Marty. Just might.

"We're looking for someone," he said.

"You are, huh? Who?"

"The monkey that burned my brother's face."

Obviously Marty had not been expecting any such straight answer. It amazed him. He took a bite out of his candy bar, and the strong odor of chocolate filled the air. He frowned menacingly.

"What makes you think you're gonna find him around here?"

"He came this way," said Chip. And then he made the pitch he had thought of. "Listen, if somebody burned one of your brothers on the face with a cigarette, would you let him get away with it?"

Marty stared at him for a moment. Then his mouth twisted in a scornful grin, and his chest swelled out.

"Are you kidding? Me and my brothers would take care of any rat that did anything like that!"

He looked past them toward the corner, and jerked his head in that direction.

"Me and Eddie, we'd find him, and when we did . . ." Chip's heart had already been beating fast, but now it jumped about four beats altogether. He glanced around wildly.

"Eddie? Who's Eddie?"

The fat man had left. The man in the black boots was still leaning against he car. He was looking their way.

"Eddie's my brother, who'd you think?" said Marty, as if the whole world was supposed to know.

Chip's head swam. Was their monkey going to turn out to be Marty Rennick's brother? And if he was, what would they do? Suppose Eddie recognized Chip and

Benny as the two kids who got in his way that night —
two kids who might recognize him? . . .

"Hey, Marty, you little bum! Gimme a bite of that
candy," said Eddie, and pushed himself away from the
car he was leaning against. Standing up straight, he
began to limp toward them.

Never in his life had Chip been glad to see anybody
limp — until now.

"Eddie just got back from Vietnam last night," said
Marty. He was trying to be very cool about it, but it
was plain he was a hero-worshiper, and Eddie was his
hero. "He knocked out a bunch of Viet Cong, and got
hit doing it."

"Gee! They hit him in the leg, huh?"

"Yeh, but he's almost well. The doc says he won't
limp hardly at all," said Marty, and try as he might to
keep his cool look, his face showed how badly he
wanted to believe it. For a second or two the tough
guy was gone. But then he covered up quickly by turning hard and cocky. "Hey, gimpy, how's the leg doing?"
he asked. Eddie grinned.

"Who you calling gimpy, you little jerk?" he said,
and took a lazy swing at Marty. It was a treat to hear
somebody call Marty Rennick a little jerk, and make
him duck a swing. "Let's have that candy," said Eddie,
and took a bite of it.

Chip thought of his cousin Fred.

"Say, we've got a cousin who knows you! He was in your outfit, even!"

Eddie glanced down at him.

"Yeh? Who's that?"

"Fred Brady."

"Brady? He your cousin?" Chip found himself basking in the hero's smile. "Sure, I know Fred. He's a good guy. We saw action together, Fred and me."

Marty was looking a lot less fierce as he took all this in. With a heady feeling that things were breaking his way, Chip pressed his luck.

"I wish Fred was here now," he said. "I'll bet he'd help us find the punk we're looking for."

"What punk?"

Marty took over. He told Eddie about the stickup in Stedman Square, and what happened to Benny. And Eddie, Chip was glad to see, looked as if he did not like the idea of the cigarette burn. Chip decided to tell Eddie the whole story. He told him how they had followed the man's tracks in the snow, and lost him at the corner of Milford and Keaney. He even told how they had tried to look for his tracks in Keaney Street, but had been chased out. With Marty standing right there, it was scary to tell that part, but he did it.

Marty laughed a tough laugh.

"That was probably Jingo Davis that threw the snowballs," he said. "You're lucky he didn't clobber you. You better not try *that* again."

He jerked his thumb at Chip and Benny.

"These guys are a cop's kids," he said, making it sound like an insult. "Their old man's a flatfoot."

Not even from Marty Rennick could Chip take "flatfoot" meekly.

"He's a sergeant," he said in a sharp voice. This got him a scowl from Marty.

"Nobody asked you," snapped Marty.

"Now, just a minute," said Eddie, and it was Marty who was getting a hard look now. "We got one cop-hater in this family, we don't need any more," he said, and Chip remembered the brother who was in jail. "In fact, you know what I was, part of the time, over in Vietnam."

"I'm trying to forget it," muttered Marty.

"Well, don't. I was an M.P.," Eddie told Chip. "Military Police. And you get a different slant on things when you're the one that's trying to hold the lid on. But anyway, what are you kids doing over here? You expect to find this guy here on Beecher Avenue?"

"Well, he came this way," said Chip. He gave Marty a quick glance. "We couldn't come through Keaney to look for him, so we're doing the next best thing and looking all around it."

"I see." Eddie thought this over. "I can't think of any guy on our street that would do a crumby thing like that, but . . ."

He looked at Marty.

"Give him a pass, and let him look." He chuckled. "Give him a three-day pass, like in the army."

Marty was outraged.

"What? Let a cop's kid stick his nose into my street and snoop around? Nothing doing!"

"I used to run that street," said Eddie, "and I'm back."

"Aw, Eddie!"

"It won't kill you."

Marty struggled with himself.

"Nuts to three days! I'll give him one day, and that's all!"

Chip managed to bargain in a small, strained voice.

"How about making it two?"

Marty looked as if he did not know what the world was coming to. He glared at Chip, and glared at his brother.

"Oh, all right, two days!" he snapped. "But that's it!"

7

Marty laid down the rules.

"Tomorrow after school, and the next day after school, and that's it," he said. "But I can tell you right now, you won't find your guy on our street. I know everyone there, and there's nobody could be him."

Eddie was grinning about the bargaining Chip had done.

"It won't hurt to let them look," he said. It was plain he did not think they had much chance of finding their man, either on Keaney Street or anywhere else. He was only having fun with Marty.

The king of the street gave his brother an annoyed look.

"If you ask me, you're getting soft in the head! Letting a kid from outside snoop around on our street — it's an insult!" he said, but that only made Eddie laugh out loud. Marty snorted, and turned to Chip.

"I'll pass the word around to my guys, so you won't get creamed," he told Chip, and dismissed him. "Okay, that's it for now. Get lost, before I change my mind!"

"Okay, Marty!" Chip was more than ready to cooperate. After the strain of the past few minutes, nothing sounded more relaxing than to put some distance between himself and Marty Rennick. "Come on,

Benny," he said, and they moved off briskly. At the corner, as they crossed over, Chip glanced at Keaney Street and felt a sudden letdown. Had he gone through all this stress and strain for nothing? He had a hunch that Marty was right, that snooping along Keaney would get them nothing.

They walked past a corner drugstore and four or five shops and stores, none of which looked very promising, and turned into Fairmont Street.

"This street is a real bust, too," grumbled Chip, as they hurried along. "He's not going to live here, because if he did he wouldn't have gone as far as Keaney on his way home."

Their whole search seemed hopeless. The odds were too great. Benny did not share his depression, however. He was excited. He blew out his breath with a loud "Whew!"

"Gee, Chip, that was really something! Boy, was I scared! Marty Rennick! Wait till —"

"Don't you say a thing to anybody about this!" snapped Chip, cutting him short. "Marty might not like it. Just keep this under your hat, understand?"

"Okay, okay. I was just —"

"Yeah, I know, you were just going to blab everything to everybody at school. Well, don't. And keep still about it at home, too, see?"

"Think I'm crazy? I won't say a word. But just the same . . . Tomorrow we'll walk right into Keaney

Street, where all the other kids are scared to go. How about that?" said Benny, all but strutting at the thought of it.

"Big deal," jeered Chip. He was feeling thoroughly depressed now. "I'll bet our guy doesn't live there. If he did, Eddie and Marty would know about it. Far as that goes, he could live anywhere," he added, and suddenly the big map of the city seemed to be before his eyes, with hundreds of streets running off in all directions. "We could walk around for a hundred years and maybe never see him. Maybe he even has a job, someplace clear across town. He might never be around at this time of day, when we can be here."

He thought about Marty, and glared over his shoulder.

"Big deal, a two-day pass to Keaney Street!" he said. "We needed that the night we were following the guy, not now!"

When they reached home, their mother was out. A note on the kitchen table said she was shopping, and would be back soon. That made things easier. No questions. Chip sat down at the table and tried to get busy on his homework. Benny opened the refrigerator.

"Want a glass of milk?"

"No," said Chip. Nothing sounded good to him just then.

Benny poured himself a glass of milk and went off to

their room to work on the model airplane he was building. Chip tried to concentrate on his algebra, but could not get his mind off their unsuccessful manhunt. The trouble was they did not have enough to go on. Remembering something his father sometimes did when he was thinking about a case, Chip took a piece of scratch paper out of his notebook and began to write down all the things they did know about:

wool plaid cap — dark green, maybe brown
tan jacket — fur collar
dark pants
big square brass belt buckle
black boots
mask
cigarette butt (fingerprints)
gun

He frowned over the list for a while, but failed to get any new ideas from it. Finally he shoved it aside and forced himself to open his algebra again.

He was working on the second problem of his assignment when all at once he dropped his pencil and stared into space. He picked up the list and studied it once more.

"Benny!"

"Huh?"

"Come here!"

The excitement in his voice made Benny come running.

"What's the matter?"

"I thought of something!"

"What?"

"Where did he buy that mask?"

Benny looked blank for a moment. Then he got the idea. Chip went on eagerly.

"You and I know what it looked like, and we're the only ones who do!" said Chip. "We've got to look around in every store in the neighborhood up there. If we can find a store that sells masks like that one, then we'll really have something!"

"Hey, Chip, that's great! How about the dime store on Milford Avenue?"

"We'll look there, and everyplace else that might sell them."

Benny let out a war whoop. Chip got up and went to the refrigerator.

"Now I'll have a glass of milk," he said.

It made all the difference in the world, having something definite to work on. He drank his milk, and thought about his father.

"Gee, I wish we could tell Pop about it, Benny."

"I wish so, too."

Chip considered for a moment, and began to discover good reasons for doing what he wanted so badly to do.

"In fact, I don't see why we can't!"

"But —"

"Listen, looking for guys and following them into alleys is one thing. Mom would lower the boom on us for that, and so would Pop. But looking for something in a bunch of stores is another thing. Even Mom couldn't get very worried about that. And we'd be better off if we *did* tell her. If she knows we're going to look around in stores, we can take more time, without worrying about getting home too late. Everything works better, see?"

"Okay, let's tell them."

"Okay. But don't talk about Marty, or Keaney Street. I still think we'd better not go into any of that!"

It was a great feeling to tell their father about how he wrote out a list of things they had to go on, and how he thought to wonder where the man bought the mask. It was great because of the way their father grinned and looked pleased with him.

When Chip told about their plan, however, his mother's first impulse was to worry. They had to expect that.

"I don't want you two getting mixed up in anything!"

"Now, dear," said Sergeant Brady, "they can't get into much trouble just looking around in stores. And it's good practice for them."

"Practice! It won't be your fault if you don't make a

detective out of Chip," she said accusingly. But Sergeant Brady gazed at his son and defended himself.

"I won't make a detective out of him," he said. "He'll make a detective out of himself. Now, I have to go in early tomorrow morning, but I'll be home early in the afternoon. If you find anything interesting, boys, you come right on home and tell me about it."

Then he added a few words based on bitter experience.

"But don't be too disappointed if you don't. It's all part of the game."

8

ON THEIR WAY up Milford Avenue the next morning, Chip and Benny took a closer look at the stores on both sides of the street than they ever had before. They had walked the street hundreds of times, but now they saw many things they had never noticed.

Besides the big dime store, there were four other places they decided they should try. Two were drugstores. One was a little novelty store that looked as if it had never made up its mind what to concentrate on. One was a place that sold cigars and cigarettes and newspapers, mainly, but seemed to have all kinds of odds and ends for sale, too.

"We'll start on Milford," said Chip, "and then we'll go through Keaney over to Beecher and look around there."

When school was out, Chip did not have to wait around for his brother. Benny shot out of the school doors as if he had been fueled up at Cape Kennedy. He was ready to go.

"Did you keep your trap shut about this today?" Chip asked sternly.

"Sure!"

"Sure?"

"Honest!"

"Well, you'd better!"

Benny still had a bandage on his cheek. It was probably the last one he would have to wear. His burn was nearly healed, and it was healing perfectly. There was not going to be a sign of a scar, which just went to show that a fellow can't have everything.

The sky had turned gray, and a few snowflakes had begun to pay a visit to the city.

"Going to snow again," said Chip, and turned up the collar of his jacket. "We'd better not waste any time."

They started with the dime store. Pushing through the swinging doors, they bustled along the aisles to the toy counter — they could have walked straight to it blindfolded — and began their search.

"Here's masks!" cried Benny, quick as usual to find anything he was looking for. He held up a pirate mask from a pile. Chip, who had started looking on the other side of the counter, hurried around to join him. They pawed through the selection, but found nothing like the mask they were looking for.

"Maybe they had some like ours and sold them," said Chip. He looked around for the nearest saleswoman. There was one at the next counter. "We're looking for a mask with red cheeks and two big teeth hanging down," he told her. "Have you had any like that?"

The woman looked up from filing her nails.

"Huh?"

Chip repeated his question.

"I don't work over there very often," she said, and glanced around, looking for another saleswoman. "Hey, Millie, these kids want to know something about masks."

"What about masks?"

Chip went over and repeated his question to the second woman. She shook her head.

"I put that stock out myself, and I don't remember one like that. Won't something else do? How about Smokey the Bear?"

"No, thanks. We wanted this special one."

"Well, you're out of luck, I guess, boys."

They left with long faces. They knew it was foolish to expect success on their very first try, but at the same time the dime store was one of their best bets. They tried the other four stores, but with no better results. Only the little novelty store had any masks, and none of them resembled the one they hoped to see. And the man there shook his head when they described it.

"Well, that's that," said Chip, as they went back out onto the avenue. "Okay, here goes for Keaney Street."

"Wow! I got the shivers," said Benny.

They walked to the corner and looked up the three blocks of the famous forbidden street. A sifting of snow speckled its dark surface.

"I sure hope Marty got the word around to everybody," said Chip. Actually, the street looked ordinary and quiet. None of Marty's gang were in sight anywhere.

With their eyes darting in every direction, they began their walk. Chip hoped there would be a store somewhere along the way, but there was not. Nothing but houses, mostly old and shabby. They had not gone far before they saw a boy they didn't know, standing between two houses, watching them with narrow eyes, but he disappeared before they could get more than a glimpse of him. All along the street they could feel eyes on them from dark upstairs windows.

"I wonder which house Marty lives in?" said Benny.

"I hope we don't find out. I could do without him today."

Chip lowered his voice to a cautious mutter.

"If you ask me, I can't see why anyone would *want* to stick his nose into this street," he declared, "but don't tell Marty!"

Keaney Street came to a dead end at Beecher Avenue. Straight across from them was a cigar store like the one on Milford Avenue.

"Let's start with that one," said Chip.

They crossed over and inspected the window. It did not look like the kind of store that went in for kid stuff such as masks.

"Well, let's ask, anyway."

The man inside was chewing on one of his own

cigars. He gave them an irritable glance. Chip told him what they were looking for. He glared down at them as if he were about to snarl at them. But then he jerked his head in the general direction of the door, and surprised them.

"Try the variety store."

"Thanks!" said Chip, and hurried out hopefully. He remembered the variety store on the corner, across the street, the one from which Marty had appeared, eating a candy bar.

But when they tried there, they found no masks.

"Masks are for Halloween," said the man who ran the place. "Other times, I don't fool with them."

Outside again, Chip and Benny exchanged a discouraged glance. Chip's big idea was beginning to lose its glamour. He looked up and down the street, and shifted his schoolbooks to his other arm. Gusts of cold wind made them hunch their shoulders, and the snow flurries were heavier now.

"Well, let's try the drugstore."

From the looks of Beecher Avenue, there were not too many other possibilities. They were heading toward the drugstore when an unwelcome sight rounded the corner. Marty Rennick. He waited for them as they walked toward him.

"I saw you go by," he said, without sounding too friendly about it.

"You mean, on your street?"

"Yeh. So what did you find out?"

"Nothing."

"I told you. I said you wouldn't. Now what are you up to?"

"We were just checking some stores."

"What for?"

"Well, you know that mask I said the guy was wearing?"

"What about it?"

"Last night I happened to think, maybe he bought it in some store in the neighborhood."

Marty's eyes flickered strangely. It was not easy to keep talking when Marty was looking like that, but Chip struggled on.

"We tried the dime store over on Milford Avenue, and a bunch of others, but no luck. Then we came over here and went to a couple. Now we're going to look in the drugstore and . . . well, that's about it."

Marty seemed to struggle with himself for a moment, but he could not resist showing off.

"I'll tell you something about the drugstore," he said. "You should have started there."

Chip caught his breath.

"You mean, they got masks?"

"They got everything. The old guy that runs it sells lots of stuff to kids, so he's always got junk like that."

Chip glanced down at Benny. At that instant Benny

seemed to consist mainly of two big round eyes. And he picked that time to open his mouth for the first time and squeak out a question.

"Okay if we look, Marty?"

The king of Keaney Street stared down at the bandage on Benny's cheek.

"Let's go," he said.

He led the way across the street and walked into the drugstore as if he owned the place. It was a cluttered store, with every counter covered with a litter of merchandise. Marty flipped his hand at the man behind the soda fountain and said, "Hi, Jake." He walked straight to a corner, reached into a box, and pulled out a mask.

"See?"

The mask was a grinning death's head. There were a couple more like it in the box, and two smaller ones that had red cheeks, but mustaches, and no teeth.

And that was all.

Chip tried to swallow his disappointment.

"Thanks, Marty, but these aren't like the one we're looking for. Well, the little ones are sort of like it, only the one we're looking for didn't have a mustache, and it had two big teeth."

In another second or two, Chip would have reminded himself that the store might have had the right kind and sold them. He would have thought to ask the man behind the soda fountain. But before he got that far, the way Marty was looking took all his attention. Chip had not described the mask yesterday when he was talking to Marty and Eddie. When he mentioned the teeth now, the way Marty took it was unmistakable. Marty knew something more than he was telling.

"What do you mean?" he asked. "What kind of teeth?"

"You know, two big teeth in front. Sort of chipmunk teeth," said Chip.

Marty hesitated. Then, once again, the desire to show off was too much for him. He jerked his head toward the door.

Again they found themselves following Marty. This time he turned into Keaney Street. Chip could imagine what Benny was thinking. Walking down Keaney Street with Marty Rennick!

They walked to the next corner and crossed over. Marty stopped in front of a brick building, stuck his fingers in his mouth, and let go with a whistle that should have shattered the windows.

One of the upstairs windows flew up. A boy stuck his head out. Chip didn't know his name, but he recognized him as a kid in the sixth grade.

"Hi, Marty. What's up?"

"You still got that mask, Danny?"

"What mask?"

"Couple days ago when I was going home, you yelled

to me and stuck your head out the window with a kooky mask on. You still got it?"

"Oh. Sure."

"Let's have a look at it."

Danny didn't ask, "Why?" Obviously Marty's gang were used to obeying orders. The window went down. They waited. Presently the door opened, and Danny came out.

"I had to hunt around for it. What do you want with it, Marty?"

He was carrying the mask in his hand. When he held it out, Chip's eyes popped.

"That's it!"

Danny looked blank, of course, because he did not know what was going on.

"What are you talking about?" he asked, and his glance darted uneasily in Marty's direction. Chip had turned to Marty. For once the king of the street was speechless. Nothing can be more startling sometimes than to score a bull's-eye.

"This is it, Marty! The exact same kind!"

Chip's voice shook with excitement. He whirled back to Danny.

"Did you buy it at the drugstore?"

"Naw. I didn't buy it anywhere," said Danny. "I found it."

"What? You *found* it?"

The words made Chip's heart pound. If Danny had found the mask, then it was no longer merely the same kind their monkey used. Now it might be the exact same one!

"Where did you find it?"

"Over on Platt Street, on the way to my cousin's."

"Platt Street! When?"

"Couple of days ago. The morning after it snowed. My old lady sent me over with some stuff for my aunt, before I went to school, and that's when I found it. Say, what's all the excitement about?"

Chip and Marty were staring at each other.

"The morning after it snowed. The morning after the stickup," said Chip.

"You heard about the stickup in Stedman Square, and the kid getting burned?" Marty asked Danny.

"Oh, sure. Say, is this the kid?"

"Yes!" said Benny.

"You remember where you found the mask, Danny?" asked Chip.

"Sure."

"Can we go see?"

Danny's small, nervous eyes consulted his leader's. Fortunately Marty's own curiosity was too much for him. The excitement of a chase, any chase, was hard to resist. He shrugged.

"Sure, let's go."

The snow and the wind made them put their heads

down as they followed Danny over to Platt Street and turned toward Beecher Avenue. He stopped in front of the third house from the corner.

"It was right here. Just a corner was sticking out of the snow."

"See? He came up our street and then cut over here," said Marty. "Probably heading for Bellville," he added, referring to another section of town a few blocks away, a real slum section. "I told you it wasn't any guy on our street."

"You're right. I wonder what made him drop it here, though?" said Chip, and as he spoke he saw something important. He saw Marty's eyes flick in the direction of the house they were standing in front of, and he saw Marty's face go deadpan.

"Maybe he jerked something else out of his pocket, and pulled out the mask with it, without knowing it," said Chip.

"Like gloves, maybe," said Benny. "One time I pulled out my mittens and lost a quarter."

"Sure, I'll bet that's it!" Marty took up the suggestion eagerly. Too eagerly. "By now his hands were probably getting cold. And that means he still had a ways to go, or he wouldn't have bothered with his gloves. I'll bet I'm right! I'll bet he lives over in Bellville somewhere."

Chip had gone deadpan himself.

"Maybe you're right, Marty," he said, but he was beginning to have other ideas. "Listen, Danny, can I borrow that mask to show my dad? We got to be getting home."

Again Danny glanced at his leader for clearance, and again Marty shrugged.

"Sure, let him have it. Come on, let's go, it's cold."

Chip put the mask in his pocket, and they all walked together back as far as Keaney Street.

"Tell your old man to check around over in Bellville," said Marty, when they reached the corner.

"I will," said Chip. "Thanks for the help, Marty."

Marty grinned sourly.

"I never thought I'd help a cop's kid do anything. I'm getting as soft in the head as Eddie," he said. "Come on, Danny."

He turned away back toward Beecher Avenue, with Danny beside him. Chip and Benny headed for Milford Avenue.

Benny was bursting with excitement and the need to talk.

"Hey, that was great, getting the mask! And how about me, thinking of the gloves?"

Chip shifted his books to his left hand and stuck his right hand in his pocket, where he carried his house key. Sometimes they needed it, when their mother was not home, so he always had it with him.

If a fellow's hands were cold, and he reached in his pocket for his house key, he could easily pull a thing like a mask out with it and not notice, especially if he was upset after blowing a stickup. And why would he pull out his key?

Because he was nearly home.

Chip put a damper on Benny's pleasure.

"Save your breath, you'll need it," he said. "We've got to get home, and fast!"

9

THE MASK was a great sensation, but explaining how they got hold of it had its pitfalls.

The trouble was, to explain about Marty and Danny they had to tell about meeting Marty the day before. That meant they had to admit they had gone snooping, looking for their monkey on street corners. In the end they confessed everything, even the part about following their first suspect, hoping to grab his cigarette butt.

To their surprise and considerable relief, Mrs. Brady did not scold them. She exclaimed over their story, and said she would have been worried sick if she had known what they were doing, but she did not really scold them. One thing that helped was the fact that their father could not conceal his pride in them.

"Benny was burned," he said to their mother. "You wouldn't want them to take that lying down, would you?"

But then he frowned at them in no uncertain way.

"On the other hand, don't you ever — *ever* — do anything so foolish again as to follow some punk into an alley, the way you did."

"Yes, sir."

"All right. Now, then. What was the number of the house on Platt Street?"

"Two-twelve," said Chip. "When Marty wasn't looking at me, I checked."

"Good." His father nodded. "If somebody lives there who might be our monkey, Marty would clam up, of course. That would be part of his code. Well, we'll see what they can tell us at the station."

Sergeant Brady was on the phone for a while, talking to men at the police station. That gave their mother a chance to fuss over them.

"All I can say is, I'm glad you're home! When it got so late, I almost sent your father out to look for you."

When he came back from the phone, his news was not encouraging.

"The house belongs to a man named Mitchell, and he and his wife are the only ones listed as living there. He owns a bar around the corner, the Beecher Tap."

"I know where it is," said Chip. "Next to the cigar store."

His mother rolled up her eyes.

"That's my boy!" she said. "Twelve years old, and he knows all the cigar stores and barrooms on Beecher Avenue!"

"Not all of them, Mom," said Chip consolingly. "Just those."

"I had them check out all the houses on the block," said Sergeant Brady, "and there's nobody listed for any of them that could be our monkey. But they put out a call to Sergeant Perelli's car, and he's going to come by here. Perelli knows that neighborhood cold. Maybe he can tell us something."

He picked up the mask again.

"Anyway, you did all right, coming up with this!"

Chip and Benny spent the next few minutes with their noses against the living room windows, watching for the prowl car. The street and sidewalks were covered now, and the front terrace was a smooth white slope.

"Here it comes!" cried Benny, catching a glimpse of the car far up the street, a split second before Chip did, and making Chip wish that just once he could see something before Benny saw it. The car swung to the curb, leaving twin curves in the snow behind its wheels. Sergeant Perelli clambered heavily out of the passenger side. He had a big paunch and walked like a tired duck. He looked sleepy, and not too bright, but their father always said not to let that fool you.

By the time the sergeant had climbed the stairs, Mrs. Brady had coffee cups set out. He gave her a fine Italian bow over his paunch, and ruffled Benny's hair and dug a thumb into Chip's ribs. They were old friends.

"What have these rascals of yours been up to, John?"

"Plenty," said Sergeant Brady. He held up the mask. "Look what they turned up. It may be the one that monkey wore."

Sergeant Perelli pursed his fat lips in a low whistle. "Not bad. How did this happen?"

Sergeant Brady gave him the details. From time to

time during the story Sergeant Perelli's sleepy eyes rolled in their heavy pouches toward Chip and Benny, and a twinkle of approval brightened them. When their father described the scene in front of the house at 212 Platt Street, Sergeant Perelli stirred in his chair like a man waking up from a nap.

"Mitchell, eh? What do you know?" he said. "Naturally the directory doesn't list his nephew yet, because he only showed up a couple of weeks ago."

His comment made them all sit up.

"Nephew? What nephew?"

"His brother's kid, from Chicago. He's been living with them, and Mitchell's got him working in his tap. Name's Tim. He's not too bright, I guess — not a dummy, I don't mean that, but no big brain, either. Mitchell uses him to run errands, like hopping over to the drugstore for cigarettes if they haven't got the kind a customer wants behind the bar, or running out for a pizza pie when one of the regulars gets hungry. There's a pizza place down the street, the other side of Platt."

"Not too bright." Sergeant Brady repeated the words, and Chip tingled as his father's own words echoed through his mind. . . . The one thing you can usually count on, as far as this kind of punk is concerned, is that he's stupid. If you can't think of anything better to do than stick up a bus driver, you have to be stupid. . . .

"How old is he?" asked Sergeant Brady.

"Early twenties, I'd say."

The two policemen stared reflectively at each other.

"Only trouble is, if Mitchell's got him working nights at his bar — unless he had a night off — he couldn't have been out riding on that bus . . ."

"We'll have to check that out."

"What's this Tim Mitchell look like?"

Sergeant Perelli's sleepy eyes almost closed.

"Average height, maybe a little better —"

"The boys say he was tall. But then he'd look taller to them, so it's hard to know."

"Slim build. Dark hair. Sallow complexion."

Sergeant Brady's sigh was halfway to a groan.

"Sounds like half the young punks we pick up. Maybe, before we go too far, it would be a good idea for Chip and Benny to get a look at him. We're hanging an awful lot on the fact that this mask was dropped in front of Mitchell's house."

"You're right. I'd hate to pull his nephew in for fingerprinting and then find we were wrong," admitted Sergeant Perelli. "Mitchell would raise the roof. And he's got connections."

His eyes glinted sideways at his friend and fellow officer.

"You sure can't afford anything like that right now, John," he added.

"You bet I can't. I'm walking on eggshells as it is," said Sergeant Brady grimly, and Chip knew they were thinking about his chances of promotion.

Sergeant Perelli stood up.

"Tell you what. I'll go up to Mitchell's tap. I got a couple of questions I can ask him, routine stuff, that won't make him suspicious. I'll see if Tim is there, and let you know. Sit tight. I'll be back."

Sergeant Brady held out the mask.

"Check this out at the drugstore, too, will you? See if they sold it, and if anybody can remember who bought it. Chip didn't have a chance to get back there and check."

Chip flushed brick red.

"I forgot!" he said miserably, but his father only smiled.

"Son, you had a busy day," he said. "You can't think of everything."

When Sergeant Perelli had gone, making the stairs creak under his weight, Mrs. Brady began to get supper ready. For Chip and Benny, what seemed like an endless wait began.

"Listen, Perelli can't fly," said their father, when they started to complain. "He's only been gone five minutes."

At another time Chip would have laughed at the thought of fat Sergeant Perelli flying, but right now he was in no mood for comedy. Mrs. Brady called to them from the kitchen.

"Come out and set the table. It'll give you something to do."

For once Chip and Benny were glad to hear the familiar order. They went at the job very deliberately, trying to make it last. But when every plate and knife and fork and spoon and cup was in place, and the napkins folded just so, Sergeant Perelli still had not returned.

"Gee, what's he *doing?*" said Chip.

"Patience," said Sergeant Brady, lolling back in his chair in the living room, trying to set an example. "If I've told you once I've told you a hundred times — in this business the first thing you need to have is patience. You spend most of your time waiting around for things to happen."

Chip flopped down in a chair and wondered if he could ever stand so much waiting around. His father grinned at him.

"It comes easier when you're older and getting paid for it," he said.

Mrs. Brady came down the hall and stood in the doorway.

"Supper will be ready in a few minutes, to help you pass the time," she told them. "I've never seen you when you couldn't eat."

She almost did that night. When she called them to

the table, both Chip and Benny picked at their food. They spent most of the time straining their ears for the sound of a car stopping out front. And when the sound came, they looked as if they were trying to get up and being held in their chairs by invisible seat belts.

"Please, can we go look?"

"Yes, you're excused."

They raced in to the living room windows and reported.

"It's him!"

By the time Sergeant Perelli made it up the stairs, they were all in the living room again. He made another bow to Mrs. Brady, folding himself over his paunch, and handed the mask to Sergeant Brady.

"No luck with this. Morry the druggist says he never had this kind in stock."

"You believe him?"

"Yes. Morry and I grew up together."

"Okay. How about the tap?"

"The kid's there. He's wearing a black turtleneck sweater, you can't miss him. I wish I could have grabbed something he handled, for fingerprints, but there's too many eyes in the place. I didn't dare."

"Of course not." Sergeant Brady pulled thoughtfully at his heavy jaw. "You say he's likely to be in and out, running errands. . . . After we finish supper, I'll get the car out and take the boys up there. We'll park across from the tap for a while."

He glanced at Chip and Benny.

"You know what I told you boys about eyewitness identifications. I don't expect you to recognize this fellow for sure, and I probably wouldn't believe you if you claimed you did. What I want to find out is, *could* it be him? If this fellow doesn't look right at all, then we won't waste time checking him out. But if he *could* be the one . . ."

"It's worth a try," nodded Sergeant Perelli. "You'll be going up there in a few minutes, then?"

"Yes."

"Okay. Good luck. And keep us posted."

The idea of "staking out" the Beecher Tap, as Benny was quick to put it, was so exciting that it was torture to have to return to the table and finish supper. Their mother was no one to be trifled with when it came to the good food she cooked for them, however; it had to be eaten.

"And don't gobble," she ordered sternly.

"That's right, plenty of time, boys," said their father, trying not to gobble himself. Somehow they managed to finish up. Mrs. Brady agreed to hold dessert until they returned.

"Be careful," she said, peering over their shoulders as they followed their father out the back door. "It's not fair, making me worry about all three of you at once!"

"Don't worry, dear. We won't be long."

As they walked out into the dark, where white drifts were already forming on the back stairs, Chip had the eerie feeling of coming full circle and being right back where the whole business began. The snow was covering everything with a good layer now, enough to make the streets look much the same as they had looked the night he and Benny went to Stedman Square to get cream for their father's coffee.

"Same kind of night," he muttered.

"I was thinking that, too," said Benny.

"So was I," said their father.

They all climbed into the front seat of the car, and

Sergeant Brady backed it out of the garage. The snow tires bit into the snow as he turned around and then headed down the drive.

"Motor sounds good now," he said. "They did a good job."

He turned into the street and drove toward Stedman Square, and none of them saw Mrs. Brady open a window, nor heard her call after them. Swinging into Stedman Square, the car circled the park, passing close by the spot where everything had happened.

"We know," said Chip, before Benny could speak. "That's where the guy burned you."

"Well, it is," said Benny, not to be done out of the pleasure of pointing out the exact spot. A bus was standing at the curb, empty. The driver was probably in the grocery store, maybe having a Coke or a carton of milk, or drinking coffee from a thermos, while he waited to start his next run back up Milford Avenue.

"Fader's better, I hear, but he's still got a long way to go," their father remarked. "Maybe I'll take you to the hospital to see him, when they say he can have visitors."

His big hands tightened on the steering wheel.

"I wish we *could* put the finger on this monkey," he said. "Every day a punk like that runs loose is liable to mean bad news for someone else."

The car rolled quietly up Milford Avenue, with the snow tires hissing slightly on the snow. The plows had not been through yet. They watched the stores go by, noting the ones they had been in, looking for masks. It seemed a long time ago, much more than a few hours. The dime store was closed now, but plenty of other places were still open, and lots of people were out, trudging through the snow, ducking their heads when snowflakes swirled into their faces.

Sergeant Brady turned into Platt Street. They all peered at 212 as they went by. There were lights on downstairs in the house, but no one in sight.

When they reached the corner, he took a look before he turned into Beecher Avenue.

"We're in luck. There's a couple of parking places right across from the tap. We'll pull in there."

He turned the corner, swung into the vacant space, and switched off the car lights. Benny climbed into the back seat to be near the window. They all stared across at the Beecher Tap, and the car seemed to throb with heartbeats. Sergeant Brady twisted around to look behind them down the avenue.

"Yes, there's the pizza place, on our side of the street. That's good."

He turned back, and looked down at his sons.

"Now," he said, "we wait. We wait, and hope somebody gets hungry for pizza."

They had scarcely settled down to wait, however, before a prowl car appeared at the corner, poking its hood out of Keaney Street. Sergeant Brady chuckled.

"There's Perelli, checking to see if we're around," he said.

The prowl car turned left and went past them on the other side of the avenue. They could see Sergeant Perelli beside Muldoon, his driver, and they knew the policemen saw them, though of course nobody did any waving. The prowl car went on to the corner, made a U-turn, and surprised Sergeant Brady by pulling up alongside them. He rolled down his window to hear what Sergeant Perelli had to say.

"John, the captain phoned your house just after you

left. Your wife yelled out the window, but couldn't make you hear, so she told them to call our car. She told the radio man we'd know where you were."

"Good for her. What's up?"

"The Commissioner's on his way to make one of his flying visits to the station house," said Sergeant Perelli in a somewhat sardonic tone of voice. The Commissioner got a lot of newspaper publicity as a man who was always on the job, and who expected everyone else in the police department to be the same way. "For once he at least phoned ahead. But the reason he phoned is, he wants to see you."

Chip could feel his father tense in the seat beside him.

"Thanks for letting me know, Mario," he said. "This could be it, one way or the other. But whatever it is, I'd hate to miss being there."

"I know. He's always talking about wanting us all to 'be in touch with the station house at all times and available at a minute's notice' — I think that's the way he says it, isn't it?" said Sergeant Perelli, sardonic again. "So we got to show him you're right on the ball."

Sergeant Brady glanced at the boys regretfully.

"I guess we'll have to give up our stakeout for now," he told them. "I'll have to drive over to the station."

Chip had never suffered from worse mixed feelings in his life. On the one hand, he couldn't have been more eager to find out why the Commissioner wanted to see his father. But on the other hand, it was excruciating to think of leaving just when they might get a look at their prime suspect.

"We could stay here and watch from the drugstore, Pop," he suggested. But his father glanced at the drugstore and then at the tap and shook his head.

"Wouldn't work. What with this snow and the dark, you wouldn't be able to see him well enough from there to tell anything about him."

Then Sergeant Brady's eyes glinted with an idea.

"Mario, will you run me over to the station house?"

"Sure."

"Would the boys be all right here if they stayed in the car with the doors locked?"

Both boys squirmed eagerly as Sergeant Perelli's sleepy eyes took in their hopeful faces. He grinned at them.

"I think they can handle it," he said. "Come on, John, we'll run you over. You know the Commissioner — he won't keep you around long. We can have you back here in fifteen, twenty minutes."

"You want to do that, boys?" their father asked unnecessarily. He shook his head in a guilty way. "When your mother finds out about this, we'll all get it! But I'll do it. Now, you lock those doors and stay put. Just watch. Chances are I'll be back before he ever shows, anyway. But be careful. Stay down out of sight as much as you can. If anybody comes along on your side of the street, keep out of sight."

"Thanks, Pop!" said Chip, as his father got out of the car.

"Yeah, thanks, Pop!" said Benny.

"Just you get that window rolled up and those doors locked," said their father, and made sure they obeyed before the police car moved away. Muldoon turned back into Keaney Street, and they were gone. Chip and Benny were alone in a car which had suddenly become startlingly silent. The boys stared at each other, thrilling to the situation, and then crouched down to eye level, showing as little of their heads as possible.

"Boy!" breathed Benny. "Wait till the kids hear about *this* — some day," he was quick to add.

10

IN SOME WAYS this waiting was not so bad as waiting for Sergeant Perelli had been, because at least something happened once in a while. The door would open, and somebody would come out, and their hearts would be in their throats for an instant. But the waiting was worse, too, because it was so agonizing to be disappointed. Each time the man who appeared turned out to be some old man, or some short fat man. Never a tall young man in a black turtleneck sweater. Other men showed up and went inside, but none of them looked right, either.

On their side of the street, the stores were dark. A single bare light bulb burned dimly in the back end of the variety store, casting more shadows than light. Minutes dragged by. It grew cold in the car. Toes began to tingle. There was no letup in the storm. Once in a while a gust of wind would start a small white twister spinning in the middle of the street. Soon a plow came through, moving fast through a snowfall that was not yet very deep, but was threatening to become so.

Across the street the door opened. It had already opened and closed so many times that Chip had lost count. He turned to watch, bracing himself for one more disappointment — and saw a man in a black turtleneck sweater. It was a heavy sweater. He had not put on a jacket.

Benny's voice fluttered with excitement as he whispered, "There he is!"

"Yes. That must be him, with that sweater."

Tim Mitchell did not have on black boots or a tan jacket with a fur-lined collar or any of the other things their monkey had been wearing. Was he tall enough? Would boots make him look taller?

"What do you think, Benny?"

"Gee, I don't know . . ."

"Neither do I," admitted Chip.

"He could be the one, I guess. But . . ."

Chip's hand closed hard on the mask he had stuffed into his pocket. Was this all they were going to have to tell their father when he got back — this maybe-yes, maybe-no stuff? Tim walked past the cigar store, chesty in the snowstorm, not letting it bother him. He stopped under the theater marquee, which was lighted up now, and looked at one of the posters. The picture had changed. Instead of a Western, a crime show was advertised. As he stood in front of the poster, Tim put his hands flat on his hips and gave his pants a hitch. A woman in the box office stared out at him with a bored expression.

Tim moved on to the next poster, reaching in his pocket as he stopped to look at it. He pulled out a pack of cigarettes, flipped one up and put it in his mouth, pulling it free of the pack with his lips. It was a piece of playacting. What had their father said? . . . "He's got a picture of himself in his twisted little mind, looking tough and cool, like some actor he saw on TV." Or in the movies. Chip watched the hunch of Tim's shoulders as he lit the cigarette, sheltering the flame from the wind. A vision of their monkey bracing himself in the aisle of the swaying bus, lighting up, seemed to blaze up in his mind.

"Benny!" he whispered, "that's the way he looked on the bus!"

"You're right! That's exactly the way! It's him!"

"Maybe," said Chip sternly, fighting to keep his head. Didn't everybody look that way, lighting a cigarette in the wind?

"What are we going to do?" asked Benny, breathing hard. He was so wrought-up and frustrated he had tears in his eyes. "Darn it, we can't just let him walk away! If only we could *prove* something, one way or the other!"

Benny had never spoken a more inspiring word. Chip was reliving the night of the stickup, with every detail flashing through his mind, and he suddenly knew how they could prove something. Tim Mitchell had walked to the corner and was crossing the avenue.

"Come on, Benny," said Chip, sliding across the front seat to the door. "We're going to find out."

"What? Gee, we can't get out of the car, Chip! Pop —"

"We've *got* to! It's the only way we can know for sure. Come on — and if I yell, 'Run!,' you turn and run!"

Unlocking the doors, they slipped out of the car. Tim Mitchell had crossed over, and was waiting on the corner for a car to pass so that he could cross Platt.

Chip and Benny ran up behind him. Chip swallowed hard, because he was almost too scared to speak. When he tried, his voice was high and shrill. But at least it was loud.

"Hey, mister!" he yelled. "Got a cigarette?"

Tim Mitchell glanced at them over his shoulder. He saw two boys standing in the snow, exactly the way they had been standing three nights ago, only one of them had a bandage on his cheek, and the other was wearing a mask.

Chip felt as if he had turned to stone. He could not have moved a muscle. If Tim Mitchell only looked at them and laughed, or told them to get lost, then he was not their monkey. But if . . .

Tim stared at them. Then his eyes widened. He whirled around, almost stumbling in the snow. His lips parted, but all that came out was a strangled sound, while bubbles of spit began to show at the corners of his mouth.

"You — you —"

Somehow Chip managed to come to life again.

"Run!" he yelled, and grabbed Benny's hand.

It was a nightmare again, only this time he was yanking Benny along while he could hear a maniac panting behind them. Only another stumble kept Tim from grabbing them before they had gone five steps.

"The drugstore!" Chip yelled to Benny, and they raced for the corner. Brakes squealed and headlights blinded them as they darted into the street, and a bumper stopped inches from their legs. Staring back over his shoulder, Chip skidded to a halt as his eyes registered the most beautiful word he had ever seen on the front of a car's hood — "POLICE." His father seemed to explode out of the rear door of the prowl car.

Chip pointed and screamed, "It's him, Pop!"

Tim had already turned, and was running back up the avenue. The prowl car's wheels spun a snowstorm into their faces as it skidded around the corner, and the spotlight pinned Tim against the wall before he had made it to the next corner. After one brief, flabbergasted, popeyed glance at his sons, Sergeant Brady pounded up the sidewalk with his service revolver out and at the ready. It was all over.

The fingerprints matched.

Benny was pretty hard to live with for a while, even though the headline over their picture read, "Chip Off

The Old Block." It was funny, but in the picture of the two boys, Benny managed to look the most important.

The headline that really counted, of course, was,

POLICEMAN NABS
SON'S ATTACKER

—

Capture Wins
Promotion To
Detective Rank

Sergeant Bresnahan might have connections, but the Commissioner knew the value of a headline. For that matter, he had already made up his mind, and that was why he had wanted to see their father.

It was just as well that the next day was Friday. One day of school like that was excitement enough. Benny was no longer the king of the fifth grade — he was the emperor. As for Chip, he told his story to a few close friends — thirty or forty — and naturally Mrs. French's ears were flapping again, so he had to tell it all over again to her, too.

The worst problem was Marty Rennick. Chip was a bit nervous when Marty got him aside on the playground. He did not know quite what to expect. But afterward, thinking it over, he was not surprised.

"I figured it might be Tim," said Marty. "But I don't rat on *nobody,*" he added, looking self-righteous.

"Besides, Mitchell's got connections," said Chip, and enjoyed the surprised look his remark caused.

"Yeh, that's right," agreed Marty. The way he said it gave Chip a chilling picture of what it must be like to live in a neighborhood like Marty's.

In the meantime, Marty was staring at him in a strange way.

"For a cop's kid, you're okay," he said, and could not restrain a lordly gesture any longer. He stuck a hard forefinger against Chip's chest. "Listen, I'm making your pass to Keaney Street permanent. You can walk up our street any time you want to!"

Looking up at Marty, Chip knew better than to brush off such an honor.

"Gee, Marty, thanks!" he said. But when he told Benny about it, he sighed.

"Now we've got to walk up Keaney Street once in a while, or Marty will get sore!"

Benny was smarter about such things. He could be philosophical about them.

"That's all right," he said. "That's a great drugstore over there on Beecher."